IBIZA
discovered

"Hey, Lilla, you're next after Duncan has finished." The barman waited for me to say something. He'd be waiting a long time. . . Tumbleweed brain. Did he just say what I thought he said?

"What do you mean?" How did he even know my name?

"Well, we have a slot for you to have a go on the open deck. It's all yours."

The fog lifted. I looked round from the guy and they were all staring at me, anxious looks on their faces. Katie had gone white and Sam grimaced. No wonder Katie had been all silent, she was shitting herself for me.

"You're on in about five minutes, if you want." I didn't know what to say. The bottom fell out of my stomach and all the Zombies I'd drunk felt like they were going to projectile all over the table. . .

Look out for more brilliant reads from Point:

JUST DON'T LET YOUR LITTLE SISTER GET HER HANDS ON THEM...

IBIZA
discovered

Janet Hoggarth

■SCHOLASTIC

MORAY COUNCIL LIBRARIES & INFO.SERVICES	
20 10 47 89	
Askews	
JCY	

Scholastic Children's Books,
Commonwealth House, 1-19 New Oxford Street,
London, WC1A 1NU, UK
a division of Scholastic Ltd
London ~ New York ~ Toronto ~ Sydney ~ Auckland
Mexico City ~ New Delhi ~ Hong Kong

First published in the UK by Scholastic Ltd, 2003

Copyright © Janet Hoggarth, 2003

ISBN 0 439 97708 8

All rights reserved

Typeset by M Rules
Printed and bound by Nørhaven Paperback A/S, Denmark

10 9 8 7 6 5 4 3 2 1

The right of Janet Hoggarth to be identified as the author of
this work has been asserted by her in accordance with the
Copyright, Designs and Patents Act, 1988.

This book is sold subject to the condition that it shall not, by way of trade or
otherwise, be lent, resold, hired out, or otherwise circulated without the
publisher's prior consent in any form of binding or cover other than that in
which it is published and without a similar condition, including this condition,
being imposed upon the subsequent purchaser.

This book is for the Prancing Pony Villa girls:
Katie "Drink Through It" Newton, Tasha "@ Pacha"
Le Marinel, Jane "Cuba Libre" Arnott, Rachel "Old Lady
Swimming" Johnson, Fi "I'm Having a Moment" Wraith
and Shelley Anne "No Knickers" Garton.
You guys rock and always will. xx

Special thanks: Neil "I'm Battered" Drummond and
Andy "Was I Run Over by a Bus?" McLennan – the
honorary hens, Elle @ KLP, Amy Townsend, Katie
Bennett, Sam Smith and all the party people we
encountered out there – Love is in the Air. . .

arrivals

I meant to ask Dad about the villa, I really did. But honestly, no really, every time I picked up the phone to call him, something happened. Mum walked in (she hates Dad) so I had to ring off, or a new tune played on the radio from Pete Tong's show and I had to write it down. Or for some unexplained reason I needed to go for a wee and then forgot. And now we are in a bit of a mess. . .

"So, Lils, is your dad meeting us or what?" That's Gemma, loon girl extraordinaire and babe of our group, scoffing some peanut-flavoured crisps. (Fave catchphrase: "I'm *not* hungover, it was a dodgy beer.") Also person most likely to go mental when I tell them that he doesn't even know we're in Ibiza, let alone supposed to be staying with him. Eeeeeeek! Gemma, Katie and Sam all looked at me as I shuffled my feet and bit my lip in what I hoped was an endearing way.

"The thing is —" I am *so* going to die — "he doesn't exactly know when we'll be arriving. . ." I sort of trailed off and hoped that somehow a massive carpet would cascade from the sky so I could sweep my uselessness under it.

"So shall we get a taxi to his villa then?" Sam was taking charge and started heading off to the taxi rank with one of the trolleys. (Favourite catchphrase: "My give-a-shitometer is on zero." Almost always directed at Gemma.)

Oh, just rip off the plaster — "Guys, he doesn't know we're coming at all." There, that was OK, wasn't it? Hmmm, maybe not. If books had sound effects, then right now you would be hearing a needle skidding off a record and the sound of wind whistling through a deserted Western town while tumbleweed was blown aimlessly and—

"What do you mean? Do you mean we have

nowhere to stay? Do you mean you fucked up?" Imagine a screeching seagull and times that by ten – that's what Gemma sounded like. *And* she spat her crisp all over the floor.

"Well . . . yes. But we can call him now." Even smiling in a sweet, "I'm so sorry, and I'll kiss your ass" sort of way had no effect. "Look, you don't know how hard it is for me to call him – I haven't spoken to him for months. You know what a waster he is, Katie." Appeal to an ally, always a good ruse. (Katie, favourite catchphrase: "I'm not sure we should be doing this. . .") "I thought it would be better to see how we could wangle it if we surprised him, that way he'll never say no, right?"

Wrong, wrong, wrong. Five minutes later, on the moby in Arrivals, talking to Dad. And I thought Gemma was loud. Dad has got a voice like gravel that has been run over by a steamroller and then torched with a flame-thrower. Yes, he smokes a million fags a day. "Philippa, have you lost your mind? This is the busiest season for me out here. I really don't need a group of your little school friends hanging round for a month doing stupid stunts in the pool and wetting the bed." I think he has forgotten that I am now seventeen, nearly eighteen and that I stopped wetting the bed last year. All those years in rehab must have warped his perception of time. He probably still thinks I am flat chested with bunches. Actually, he's got a point there. . .

"Dad, please don't leave us on the streets. We might get raped or mugged. You know what the mingers are like on their way to San An. They're like Vikings. . ." etc, etc, blah, blah, etc. But he was impervious to my wheedling, wanting us to stay in a grotty apartment in town – nice. This I hadn't anticipated, I thought he might be a bit pissed off with the lack of a phone call, but not this total shirking of fatherly concern. As I held the phone away from my ear (he was going on AGAIN: irresponsible, thoughtless, no regard for privacy, zzz) and caught sight of Sam and Gem looking like lynching was too good for me, I had an idea. Katie looked like she was about to burst into tears – this wasn't what she'd expected – just what I needed!

"DAD!" I shouted to get his attention. The only way, according to Mum, that ever works is to shout. "Mum said you would be like this!"

Sound of choking and silent fuming. I expect his head looked like it had been boiled. "Your mother said *what*?"

"She said that you would be so wrapped up in

yourself that you wouldn't even have time to say hello, let alone let us stay with you. . ." More tumbleweed. And whistling wind. Maybe a lone horseman. . .

"Get in a taxi! I will not have your mother telling lies about me!" He was pissed off big time. Nice one – sometimes it's handy that they really don't get on. "The minute you get here, you are going to call her and tell her you are at the villa and staying with me, for the meantime. Is that clear?"

I heard beeping coming from my phone. "Dad, we have to go. My battery's about to die."

"Phil, there is one thing I need to warn you about. You—" It went dead.

"Right, we've got some beds! Don't look so pleased, everyone." Katie just looked worried. This wasn't what I'd promised her.

"We would have had some beds if you'd sorted this out BEFORE we left England. Now your dad is going to hate us on sight and make our lives a misery. And there's no way we can gatecrash any of his celeb parties." Aha, Gem, get to the point.

"Listen, if I'd rung and asked beforehand, he probably would have said no flat out, and we couldn't even afford a week in a fleapit here, let alone a month. This way is best, honestly." They harrumphed for a bit as we waited for a taxi. For the first time since we collected our bags I felt a sense of relief. The sun was just setting over the hire-car car park and the palm trees were wafting in a honey-scented breeze. We all seemed to calm down and drink in the smell, letting the warm air soothe away any further nit-picking.

"You can just feel the atmosphere from here, can't you?" sighed Sam. She was looking dreamy and Gem was laughing at her. I knew what she meant. Ibiza had a way of making you drunk without any alcohol.

"Don't you mean you can smell the drink!" and Gemma cocked her head towards a taxi emptying its carload of passengers at Departures. It was five blokes and they looked wasted. You really could smell the fumes from where we were, ten metres away. They fell over their cases and were slurring really badly. Urgh! Typical Brits abroad. To be avoided at all costs.

Their driver cruised up to the taxi rank. Sam took charge again and soon we were sat inside with the windows well and truly wound down to fumigate it. I sat in the front to direct the driver and thought about how we had got here, us four in the taxi on the way to some sort of adventure (well, we were like the Famous Five, except we didn't have Timmy the dog). And we wouldn't be drinking lashings of ginger beer, hopefully buckets of Sea Breezes and Margaritas – Gemma would make sure of that. It seemed an age since we planned this trip, but it was only two weeks ago. Cue the shimmering effect as we go back in time. . . Hang on, what did Dad mean, *for the meantime*? Shimmer, shimmer. . .

chapter
one

What can I say, except that I thought the day would never arrive that Katie finally told that "Prince William" loser where to go. Of course I didn't say that, what I did say was, "Katie, I think you did a very brave thing. Everyone knows you're too good for him." And I stroked her hair while she sobbed into a copy of 19 magazine, getting some new boy band all wet.

"What do you mean, everyone?" she wailed, looking up from Kieren Lubbock who was now covered in snot and tears.

"Er, well, me really. Just me, and maybe one or two of the girls at school." I omitted to mention her parents and her little brother, Ant, who thought Tom was, in his words "an amoeba on Jabba the Hutt's bum". (Nice analogy, though I worry how he knows what Jabba's bum looks like. I always thought he was freeze-framing the film to leer at Princess Leia in the gold bikini. . .) How could she not have noticed that everyone hated him? They say love is blind, but she must have been deaf as well not to have heard the gagging that went on whenever she mentioned his name at school.

They had broken up once before but Tom had managed to worm his way back in that time, convincing her it was only 'cos he loved her so much that he spied on her while she was at the cinema. Whatever. This time, I felt it was fatal. Hopefully this would mean Katie would do the drinking, snogging and vomming of a newly single girl – the classic Get Over Him ritual! I couldn't wait to plan some nights out. . .

"I had no idea everyone thought that. What are you looking so pleased about?" she whimpered.

"Nothing, honest." I wiped the smile off my face

and all thoughts of bachelorette outings vanished from my head. Almost. Give boys a massive body-swerve until they all grow up and abandon their spot farms and learn to wear deodorant. Aim high, I say. Real men are where it's at, not schoolboys. Come on, they are *children*. . .

We were slouching in Katie's bedroom. It was the last week of school and we didn't have any more exams. Tomorrow was Friday and that was the official last day, for ever. I couldn't wait. School didn't exactly float my boat. Don't get me wrong, I'm no rebel – I go to lessons, do the homework (well, copy Katie's), got a place at Uni depending on me getting the grades, and turn up mostly on time, but I sort of checked out of there years ago. It's like someone else goes in my place and reports back telling me what's going on, what essay to write and when to turn up for exams.

"I cannot believe it's over, though." Aaah, the record started up again. "I mean, nearly a year just wasted. I feel so sick and stupid. . ." Time for more tears, but no, she didn't. She just stared at his picture on her bedside table and picked it up.

Tom Philipps was good-looking if you liked that public school Prince William type of guy. And not many people I know do. Katie met him when our school, Ryedale High School for Girls (yes, it *is* posh), had a disco and bussed in a load of boys from the neighbouring boys' school, imaginatively called Ryedale High School for Boys. It was love at first sight for Katie – well, she was only sixteen, what do you expect?

"I don't understand where it all went wrong," she whinged, tracing her finger over his really uncool bouffant hairdo.

Let *me* tell you where it all went wrong, missy. It went wrong the minute you sucked face with that munter. Sorry, I have Tourette's when it comes to Tom. What actually came out of my mouth was: "Katie, there really is no point picking over the carcass of your relationship." Can't you tell I am worldly-wise in these matters? "You're just going to feel worse. It is over. End of matter. Get on with life. Tom's a dick and now you know it, so you should be glad you spotted it in time before you really came a cropper and went to med school as his girlfriend and never made any new friends." *Controversial. . .*

Katie just looked at me as if I had grown a beard. Let's just say I probably shouldn't have said what we had all been thinking for the last six months. I decided to go before she battered me to death with the ridiculous bear Tom had bought her for Valentine's Day. Mr Snuffles he was called. Finger, say hello to my throat.

"I'll see you tomorrow at school, yeah?"

"Lilla, it isn't a tap, you know. I can't just turn off how I feel instantly." She caught my blank look. "Oh, whatever. . ." But what did I know about love? About as much as I know about naked darts, so loads then. The bottom lip was going again. But she knew I was right about Tom, and now she just had to face it again, like she had done about two hours earlier. . .

We had decided to go to the cinema that day in the early evening. I was waiting for Katie in a buzzing bar full of chrome, leather and boys with too much aftershave on. It was only seven pm and already it was packed with after-work people and students from the Tech. I had bought two Cokes and was waiting for Katie near the bar. Just as she walked in, I heard this loud, braying, hideous sound that only a familiar horse-faced prince looky-likey could make. Tom couldn't see me 'cos he was too busy ogling some Britney wannabe's tits while his group of moronic mates egged him on. The girl was tossing her mane of streaked and

Domestos blonde hair everywhere and laughing in a tittering, "I'm so blonde and gorgeous and look at my tits" way. I almost got up and gave her my hoodie to cover them.

Unfortunately, Katie came up just at that moment, and followed my gaze. Her face went grey, and then Tom went in for the kill, nibbling the girl's ear, looking down her top while stroking her thigh. All at the same time – what a talented boy. Britney loved it for some reason. It was all over when Katie tapped him on the shoulder and threw her Coke in his face. "That'll cool you down!" she hissed, her voice cracking only once. Then she ran out, I still had my Coke, Tom was spluttering and going ape, and I thought it was a shame that Britney had missed out, so I "spilled" mine down her top and legged it.

"That was brilliant, Katie. You were sooo cool." I caught up with her round the corner by the Hellenas Kebab Shop. She was shaking. One thing you should know about Katie is that she's quiet and not prone to doing things like that. She looks so small and gentle in a vulnerable way, but with this incredible smile, eyes like caramel and long real-blonde hair. None of this Domestos rubbish. I can't remember her ever losing it. She spotted a bus and grabbed me. "I'm going home. Will you come?" Like I had a choice. . .

Do you really want to hear the ins and outs of Katie's "relationship" with Tom? It's dead boring, honest. You'll be asleep before the end of the paragraph. Nutshell: he's a control freak who doesn't like her having an opinion on anything from the colour of her own knickers to world peace. He wants to see her when *he* wants and if she isn't on tap for him, he throws his toys out of the pram. No, I don't understand either.

"I can't believe he hasn't phoned," she cried as we sat on the bus, "just to explain. I hate him."

You and me both. Two seconds later the phone kicks in and I can hear a stream of grovelling – pathetic. Then when that didn't work: "She's your what? Your COUSIN?" Why am I surprised? Boys are so shit at lying – why bother if you haven't the imagination to at least come up with something that sounds realistic. Incest is best – so he *was* a member of the royal family. . .

Katie was white with rage, staring at her silent phone like it was a twatty boy.

"Let's stop at the shop and get some Häagen Dazs and fat Coke. *Not Another Reality TV Show* is on at eight. If we hurry we'll catch it."

"I feel too sick to eat anything."

"Even Belgian Chocolate and Cookies & Cream?"

"Yep," she sniffed, a tear squeezing out of her right eye.

"Oh, Katie!" See – body-swerve boys. That way you won't ever refuse Belgian Chocolate. This was serious. . .

chapter

Ibiza – the island of sin, sin and sun. It never rains (well, rarely) and it's open twenty-four hours. Perfect for us then, after a year of hard slog doing A levels (ahem). I had wanted to go there for as long as I could remember – on my own, without rentals. Of course I had been there before to visit Dad in his villa when I was twelve and fifteen. But that was sanitized: no clubs, no boys, no dancing; just sunbathing, water sports and eating. He works out there for the summer most years. You see, my dad, Steve Wheeler, is a sort of famous DJ. He used to be *really* famous back in the mists of time. I had a "minder" when I was out there (all two weeks of it) and Dad did make the effort, when he had time and wasn't suffering from a monster comedown.

For the last year all he's been famous for is being in *OK Magazine* – I think it was his agent's idea of keeping up his profile. ("My Rehab Hell" or "How Drugs Killed My Marriage" or even "How I Nearly Lost My Daughter" – yes, that one was about me, and no, I refused to have any pictures taken.) I can tell he hates it and *I* think it's sooooo uncool, but he's trying for a comeback and it keeps him in the press for his recovery rather than his falling over at awards ceremonies and getting in punch-ups. Steve Wheeler, once big-time Ibiza DJ Robber Baron, now *OK Magazine* shareholder. He still does parties and clubs, but he just isn't as popular as he once was. There are younger, more "street" DJs moving up the ranks. I bet it irks him.

Now, the headline about the marriage, that isn't strictly true. The griff on the rentals: he left Mum and me years before his drug-taking and party lifestyle became his trademark, getting him all the best clubs in Europe. I don't think marriage was really him. They married too young, he got famous for his Ibiza involvement, he left, broke Mum's heart and she took ages to get over it. She's bitter and hates the way he's so crap with me. But I have to say, he's improved in the last year, not quite so mad any more, but there's no point telling Mum that. She hates any mention of Ibiza, blaming it, the music and DJing for the decay of her marriage. And just saying Dad's name makes her face pucker like she has a bad taste in her mouth. But that story is best left alone.

There is an unspoken ban on me playing "Steve's Music" at home too loud. She doesn't tell me to switch it off, just goes round the house banging things and pursing her lips, so for a quiet life I obey. I had a go on Dad's decks when I was fifteen and I got bitten by the bug. Dad gives me money every Christmas and birthday and I saved and saved for a year until I had enough for a second-hand pair of Technics and a crappy mixer. But I couldn't keep them at home; Mum would spit the dummy – she has no idea I love DJing, it would break her heart all over again. Katie suggested I keep them at hers, in her room. At first her mum said no – she didn't like going behind Mum's back. But when I explained that I wasn't allowed to mention Dad's name at home (I laid it on thick), all music was banned and how I felt I was missing out on a valuable life experience, blah, blah, etc, she bought the ticket.

Now I'm round Katie's quite a lot, on the ones and twos, spinning tunes in her room while she watches *EastEnders* downstairs. Sometimes she'll listen, but Katie wouldn't recognize a good cake mix, let alone one of mine. She likes the music, but I think for her to listen while I am up there, quite literally lost in music, is a bit boring, especially at first when I couldn't mix and her room sounded like it was being invaded by a herd of buffalo. But I am much better now, well, not much, but it doesn't sound as bad as it did before!

That's when I decided to start clubbing too – you need to if you want to listen to unreleased music. But who to go with? Katie wouldn't come – she said we'd never get in. She was a bit scared, I could tell and she was probably right, but I had to give it a go. Mum was away at Auntie Claire's one night and shock horror, I was abandoned. Call Childline! The devil on my shoulder was like: "Hey, why not go down to Milo on your own? Dave Leatherall's playing." (My hero.) "Who will know? Mum isn't here. You have enough money for a cab home. Do it, do it, do it!"

So I did. Yikes!

I was wearing my best outfit: red hipster flares with distressed bleach marks so they looked worn, a chunky brown leather belt, tight strapless black top – I looked eighteen, I knew I did, especially now I'd had my long brown schoolgirl hair cut into an elfin crop. The wait in the drizzle, getting lost down a windy corridor and being scared on my own was worth it: the whole place was a writhing mass of arms, heads, handbags. People's faces were turned to the DJ booth at the far end of the cave-like room, arms waving, showing appreciation, looking like they were in heaven and Dave was the God who had taken them there.

I was oblivious to all the sweaty bodies around me, when I felt something wet on my foot and saw this girl retching. Enter Gemma. She looked up, a big grin on her face, and then someone behind grabbed her and smacked her across the back of the head – that was Sam. "I am soooo sorry!" Sam shouted in my ear. "Did she get any on you?"

I just stared at them. Gemma was laughing like a loon. "Yes, she puked on my foot!" I pointed to my red suede trainers, stained with something looking suspiciously like a diced carrot or two. I tried not to look too closely.

"Gemma, you're foul sometimes! Here, come with us and we'll wash it off in the loo." She grabbed my hand and dragged me up the stairs round the corridor, up some more metal stairs and along another corridor with purple curtains either side, finally ending up in a queue. In the half-light of the corridor I could see Gemma was really pissed or something else, I wasn't sure. She was beautiful. Black hair all thick and curly, stick thin, cocoa latte skin – she looked like she should be in a pop video. I could see her flat tummy peeking out from under her denim boob tube and she had her bellybutton pierced. Sam was more conventional-looking with a heart-shaped face, freckles, cropped hair and wide-set brown eyes. She had a spot underneath her nose that she had tried to cover up, not very successfully. Apart from that she looked great. She reminded me of Bambi because she was also really tall with skinny legs. She wasn't drunk, or was covering it up really well.

"I'm Sam and this pig-dog is Gemma." Gemma looked at me and smiled.

"Sorry about your trainer," she said, looking like she meant it, and lit up a fag.

"That's OK; they're only my best ones. I'm Lilla."

"Who are you here with?" Gemma stabbed her fag at me nearly catching my hair alight.

"No one." They looked in awe of me, which made me feel pretty cool, 'cos I did feel a bit of a twat on my own, but wouldn't have admitted it. Norma no mates. And so began our friendship, outside that loo, in the queue with lots of wasted girls putting on lipstick and everyone smoking. It was ace.

chapter

three

Fast forward two years and we're fine-tuning our holiday to Ibiza in Café Baroque, our hang-out – candles, fairy lights, cool salsa house music and skinny lattes. All winter we'd talked endlessly about it, I'd even let them in on the secret of my dad being Steve Wheeler, fuelling the fire of Gemma's overactive imagination. "Wow, we can go to all his celeb parties if we stay with him!" I still hadn't mentioned that I'd yet to ask him if we could have the small flat attached to the farmhouse; a minor detail I could sort nearer the time, even though we were going in two weeks.

"There's one thing I need to ask you two," I said, not sure how they would take it. "You know my friend Katie?" They nodded. "Well, she's in a bit of a fix. . ." And I told them about the recent dramas. They'd only met her a few times 'cos we didn't all go to the same school. They went to a comp in Camden, quite a way from us. They thought Katie was a bit of a mouse, but she just needs time to open up. "Basically, I think she should come, it would stop her getting back with that arse, and she needs a holiday from herself. She's been too serious lately."

"Why are you asking?" Sam said. "We're staying with your dad, it's your shout." She was right, there was nothing they could really do, but I thought it only polite to ask.

"She won't whinge all the time, will she?" Gemma pouted from behind her wraparounds, hiding from yet another hangover. Sorry, *dodgy beer*.

"Gemma! Don't be so rude!" Sam chided like her mum.

"But she doesn't seem the clubbing type."

"No, but she's great once you get her going and this holiday could do that for her. She'll be fine, I'll smack her if she moans too much!" Katie was in. Now all I had to do was persuade her she wanted to come. . .

It took a few goes, but my sales pitch was class. "We'll be in the hills so we can get away from the buzz when we want some peace; we've got our own key to the flat; it'll be free; all we need is spends and flight money; there's a pool; all the fit boys go out in the trendy Old Town not far from us; we're miles away from minging San Antonio and have no need to even go there; Dad's always out; Gemma and Sam REALLY want you to come. . ." Her mum thanked me when I left that evening – she wanted Katie to get over Tom as much as I did. Now, final task, telling Mum, something I had put off for months. . .

Pursed lips, mouth sucking a lemon, looking at me like I was letting her down: "But Philippa, darling, *Ibiza?*" Mum spat it out like it was the name of a leper colony. "You want to go and have a whole month out there? With your father? Darling, he won't look after you. You'll have to fend for yourselves, you know what a selfish man he is." Yes, Mum. "I thought you were getting a holiday job here?"

"That's the idea, Mum. To do our own thing — we don't *need* to be looked after, I am nearly eighteen!" She could be as dim as him sometimes. I ignored the job question.

"Yes, but that terrible TV programme, darling. Those . . . oiks being sick in the street. Imagine if one of them was sick all over you, darling, on your Manolos." She didn't know I was going with someone who already had been. . .

"Mum! We will not be going anywhere near San Antonio. I do realize that it's a vomitorium and filled with mingers, we're too sophisticated for that."

That's the thing with Ibiza: for the uninitiated, it's full of pissed English tourists who shag in alleyways and hurl chunks in the gutter. And, of course, San Antonio is EXACTLY like that, worse, in fact. Men roam in packs, dressed in England shirts with faces like ferrets, downing pint after pint until they can't hold their wee in. Girls stagger around on white heels, perms bobbing as they cackle to their bunch of mates, all in uniform: miniskirts, boob tubes, handbag, ankle chain. I know I am being a snob, but I'm not lying — it's all there on telly. But "Comparing Ibiza Town to San Antonio is like comparing St Tropez with Skegness. No contest."

And luckily for us, Dad's place was in the hills behind the cool part of Ibiza – Ibiza Old Town.

"Now St Tropez, Philippa, why don't you go there? So much more classy. Someone at work has a holiday home there, they know people, I could get a beautiful room in a house for you and your friends . . . they have a son, your age." See what I mean? Obsessed with St Tropez. Mum would rather we actually went there with all the Rahs, where everything costs a million Euros and the only nightclubs are full of ageing millionaires feeling up young gorgeous women. No ta.

It's too late for St Tropez now, we're hurtling towards my dad, who is no doubt silently fuming that I am barging into his pulling palace. Mum grudgingly gave her blessing, but really, she could hardly stop me from seeing my own dad, could she? And she knew Katie was coming, so that always made things easier – she loves Katie. Katie is a nice girl who has a *boyfriend* (not any more). I think Mum is convinced I'm a lesbian.

Roundabouts, the odd supermarket and huge billboards advertising the DJs, superclubs and good times passed us by – everyone craned their necks to get a proper look at Ibiza Old Town as we skirted round the edges on the way to Dad's villa.

Sam leaned over to the front. "Lilla, why'd you bring your record box all the way here? Were you hoping to get a gig or something?" she half-joked.

It was a good question and not one I could easily answer. I *think* I brought it to have a go on Dad's decks hoping he would be out an awful lot, and maybe, just maybe, see if I could get a job playing somewhere, anywhere. To be honest I hadn't really thought that far. Before I could speak, Gemma got all overexcited and the records were quickly forgotten.

"Look, there's Pacha!" she shouted, as we went over a roundabout. We all looked for the club with whitewashed walls and flood-lit palm trees while the last rays of the sun caught the roof, casting shadows and warming the white to a more Moroccan terracotta. "Ohhhh, we have to go there!!!" she squealed. It did look spectacular, like a giant pop star's villa, but obviously a lot more tasteful.

As Pacha slipped away behind us until we were ready to visit it properly, the higgledy-piggledy town rose up from the harbour to meet the sky. The sprawling mass of whitewashed and sandstone buildings was punctuated by the greenery of palms, the dying rays catching shutters and chimneys, bathing the ancient city wall in rich amber light. Not a high-rise or hideous modern hotel complex in sight.

After about three more roundabouts, we arrived at the village where my dad lived: the excellently named Jesus. It was just a strip either side of the main road, but there was a good mini-market that sold lots of nice fresh fruit and veg and also the most important ingredient: enough booze to keep a small army of boy bands afloat for years. The café where Dad used to take me for breakfast had expanded to take over what used to be the chemist next door. Candles flickered underneath the blue and white stripy canopy, lighting up people's faces smoking, chatting and drinking as we went past in the taxi, up the hill, round the bend past the garage and turned off on to the familiar dirt track.

We were bumping up a steep hill, past fields either side dotted with bent olive and almond trees, twisted by the wind blown in off the sea season after season. The sun had almost set – it was about nine at night and at the top of the hill I could make out lights dancing in between the palms and dense greenery of Dad's villa. Everyone had gone quiet, even Gemma, 'cos the view was awesome. Behind us the whole valley stretched out up to the hills on the other side where the sun dipped below the black jagged line of the horizon. "Wow," whispered Katie, craning her neck. We turned off the track on the left, up another smaller track about twenty metres long shielded by trees and shrubs creating a tunnel, and there at the end, behind gates, was the villa, illuminated with up-lighters.

"Oh my God, it looks like Pacha!" Sam was impressed. I'd forgotten how striking Dad's pad was. It was an old farmhouse, a *finca*. He had added the upstairs and the spare wing on when he bought it in the early nineties. The taxi dropped us outside the gate and I pressed the buzzer. After a minute the gates silently parted and we trooped in. I was feeling a bit sick. The last time I'd seen Dad was in March and he'd seemed a bit distracted. I was convinced he'd wanted to tell me something, like he was going back into rehab. This was something I dreaded 'cos it would mean he'd been up to his old tricks, getting in a mess, and I preferred him sober, thank you very much. So we had spent the weekend at his house in Hertfordshire, both of us being polite and skirting round what it was he really wanted to say, or didn't.

I was also a tad scared of the potential bollocking. Dad could be fierce, and he didn't care whom he did it in front of. I suddenly felt twelve. Katie held my hand. "Oh God, Lilla – he's going to go mad," her voice wobbled. "What will we do if we really are in the shit?"

"Katie, stop fretting. It's bad enough that I'm worried without you moaning too. He's not going to go mad. He'll be fine." Hello? Are you insane? Of course he was going to eat us all alive, but I couldn't tell her that or she'd have refused to come in. I walked up the little steps at the front of the house and through the already open double French doors, into the living room, paved with ancient stone slabs. "Dad?" I could hear chill-out tunes coming from somewhere. Shitola, now I was going to get a mouthful.

"We're in the kitchen." We? The light from the kitchen spilled into the living room and stopped me from tripping over a pair of high heels sticking out from under the maple-wood coffee table. Aha, bad mood explained. I was not looking forward to this at all. Could we creep out? Katie pushed me forwards.

"Watch the shoes," I warned. Dad was sat at the enormous chunky farmhouse table which was covered in food, all in terracotta dishes, all looking yummy. It was an age since we'd last eaten. There was a woman with her back to us, stirring something in a giant steel pan on the ridiculously massive six-ring Aga, her long black hair caught up in a messy topknot.

"Well, hello, trouble." Dad's bad mood had obviously dispersed – he's like Jekyll and Hyde sometimes. I suppose you'd say he's a handsome man: black hair cut really short, brown skin, not too many lines, apart from a few round the eyes and mouth – his hard-living lines he calls them. His most extraordinary feature is his eyes – azure blue. With Irish rentals, no wonder he is such a hellraiser, or a retired one. The woman turned round when he spoke. She was exotic-looking, quite young and had the best skin I had ever seen – coffee with chocolate flake freckles. She was petite with huge bazoomas – accentuated by her peasant-style top. Dad is deffo a boob man. No, horrid image in head – banish it!

"This is Lena." She smiled a really genuine smile – very open and friendly. I had only really been introduced to one of Dad's girlfriends before, a Swedish air hostess who had draped herself over him whenever he sat down for two seconds. I had read about the others in the tabloids though – they were usually blonde, thick and some sort of dancer/model/weathergirl type. Lena seemed none of the above. I introduced the gang.

"I made some supper; I thought you'd all be hungry after your long trip here." Her accent was from London, I guessed, but she looked like she was from somewhere far more interesting. "Just dump your bags, we can sort them out later." I made sure my record box was well-disguised under Katie's denim jacket, I didn't want any questions from Dad.

"Do you all eat fish? I have vegetarian stuff too if not. Sit down."

Dad poured the wine on the table into some glasses. We all took one, but he didn't. Lena handed him a cranberry juice. Flippin' heck!

The food was amazing – grilled tuna steaks with lots of salads; black beans marinated with red onions, garlic, basil and lots of oil and vinegar; ratatouille. Lena was an amazing cook.

"So, why didn't you call before you left the UK?" asked Dad, raising his eyebrows. Oh, here we go.

I didn't want to have an argument about the same old same old.

Gemma looked at me and then spoke very quickly. "We did have somewhere to stay, a friend of a friend of my parents had a place and we were going to stay there in San Antonio, but it, errr . . . it burned down. We only found out when we got off the plane. I had a message to call them." Sam and Katie were goggling and I was trying to shut my mouth to stop the flies making it their home. "Lilla, I mean Philippa, was going to call you to come and visit when we had settled in, but not to stay or anything. She didn't want to get in the way. . ." Shut up, Gemma, before you say something really stupid.

"Really?" You can't kid a kidder. "I got the impression this was first choice, Philippa. You didn't mention this burnt-out place on the phone earlier."

"That's because— Ow!" Gemma shouted, as Sam kicked her under the table.

Dad looked at me, his eyes twinkling, enjoying winding me up. Sadist.

"Does it matter? We're here now. Please can we stay?" I took a chance and waited for him to say something. He didn't.

"Oh, Steve, stop teasing them!" Lena chided.

"So we *can* stay in the flat," I said hopefully, an angelic look on my face.

"Not exactly," he said looking cagey. "That's Lena's office now. She moved in a while back." Oh, thanks for telling me. . .

"So where then?" I waited. "Dad!"

"Steve, you *are* mean!" Lena cried. "I've managed to find you girls somewhere really nice to stay instead, just up at the back about five minutes from here. We can pop over in the morning."

And roll the opening credits for the movie of our holiday. . .

chapter
four

"I hope this place is nice tomorrow," said Katie as we lay in the dark, staring up at the stars through the skylight in the old beamed roof. "I really thought we were going to have to go home for a minute earlier. I think Gemma and Sam would have killed you." But luckily Lena had spared my life. She's a club promoter; that's how she met Dad last summer. But she wasn't the usual coked-up freak show, I had a feeling Lena was different, especially if Dad was doing an *OK* shoot with her – that was another reason why we had to be out of the way tomorrow. *OK* were showing up mid-morning to do yet another feature on Dad – purlease! I have no idea why he does them if he hates it all so much, but it was Lena's idea and she was pretty excited about it. *I* think it's naff, but we won't go there. . .

One of the DJs at Lena's club night, Nectar (Jules French – really famous in clubland, well, *I* knew who he was), owned the villa in the next almond grove over at the back, but he pulled out of the line-up two days ago. He had been in a near-fatal car crash in Birmingham and was going to be out of action for the rest of the season. We were going to stay in it for freeeeeeeee!!!! I know I'm evil, but I was glad he had been in the crash! Bolt of lightning, anyone?

I lay dreaming of the villa. Jules was a DJ – his decks would be there. Bring it oooon. We could have parties after the clubs shut, inviting people back, all of us being the best hostesses with the mostesses, but betting Gemma would out-most all of us put together. And there would be people there who would be wowed by my DJing skills, I would be asked to DJ in a club, possibly Space on the Terrace, warming up for Fatboy Slim. "Wow, Lilla, you're amazing. That mix you did with S Club and Pinky and Perky was mind-blowing!" Everybody was cheering and had their hands in the air, when a siren went off . . . urgh. S Club???????? A rooster was crowing in what seemed like my inner ear.

Katie groaned and stuck her head up out of the covers. "What time is it?" she croaked.

"Time to change my taste in music." S Club – that worried me more than dreaming of playing strip snap with Mr Harris, my maths teacher, and that dream had scarred me for the rest of last term. I had no idea he had a tattoo. . . All the shutters were closed and the shafts of light from the skylights captured millions of dust motes, making them dance. "We need to get going, like now, before we appear in *OK* as sulky teenagers."

Gemma and Sam were lifeless lumps under covers and pillows in the living room. "Come on, get up." Groaning and shuffling followed suit.

Dad was up and making breakfast in the kitchen. "Do you want a fry-up, ladies?" he asked clapping his hands together as we trooped in, hair still wet from the shower. But before we could answer a resounding "Yes!" Lena stopped him.

"Steve, I spent ages cleaning the place last night

before bed for the OK shoot, a fry-up will just create a mess." She gave him a Look. It was weird seeing Dad getting nagged and taking it!

"Well, I guess that's off. We've got some croissants and raisin bread instead."

When Lena reached into the fridge to get the butter, he rolled his eyes at me and shook his head. I was glad we weren't here for the shoot, looked like Lena had it all planned down to the last coffee mug arranged artistically on the dresser. We'd really be in the way for all the cheesy "At home with Steve Wheeler and his stunning girlfriend Lena Whatsit" quotes.

After breakfast, Lena agreed to whiz us over to the villa before the photographer turned up. We were carrying our stuff out to the car when Dad spotted my record box.

"Hey – what's this?"

Oh, bollocks. I pretended not to hear him and carried on slinging bags into the boot, hoping he would give up and leave it. But he was like a terrier with a juicy bone.

"Come on, Philippa, I asked you a question. Don't just ignore me." Uh-oh, he was already starting to sound tetchy. Maybe Lena hadn't given him his shot yet. . .

"What does it look like?" I tried the defensive obnoxious teenager approach.

"A record box, smart arse. What are you doing with one of those? Not very practical for keeping lipstick in, is it?" Yeah, ha ha. . .

"No, but it's good for keeping my records in." I faced him, hands on hips and head on one side, the familiar feeling in my tummy signalling that any minute now we would be at each other's throats.

"I hope you're not doing what I think you're doing," he said in his "I'm about to blow a gasket" voice.

"And what would that be, Dad? Spinning some tunes? Having a laugh?"

"In Ibiza? You never said anything about this before." I shrugged, not wanting to tell him a thing, wishing I had bluffed my way out of it. "DJing out here isn't as easy as it looks, you know." Oh, here we go. . .

"Oh, really. You think I don't know that."

Lena and the girls had finished loading up the car and didn't know what to do. I could see Katie going white – she knew what Dad was like in a full-blown rant.

"How can you? You don't know what the scene's like, you're only a kid still."

"Dad, I'm the same age you were when you started."

"Yes, but I'm a bloke, I could take care of myself . . . it's different for you."

Oh, right, I get it. I'm a girl, so therefore I'm shit. It all made sense. And he *didn't* look after himself – he spent a year in rehab, for Christ's sake!

He looked at me, eyes blazing, getting ready to change up a gear and let rip with his foghorn voice and have a proper go. But I wasn't going to let him have the satisfaction, not in front of my friends.

"Fine, you just believe what you want to. I'm going now. I'll see you around." And I climbed into the car shaking with anger, the effort of not shouting at him almost swallowing me whole.

"Philippa, don't you walk away from me!" It made no difference; he was determined to rant anyway.

"Steve! Leave it!" Lena touched his arm. He shrugged her off, but she blew out her cheeks in a "Don't you start on me" gesture. "We're going now, make sure you clean up before they get here."

He ignored her.

"Steve! *OK* will be here in an hour and the breakfast things are all over the kitchen!"

"For fuck's sake! I'll do it!" And he turned round and stalked off, not before I heard him mumble, "Bloody *OK Magazine*," under his breath.

"Bye, Mr Wheeler!" Gemma shouted at his hastily retreating back. Sam hit her – what a great start to the first day!

We all sat in silence for the five-minute drive to the villa. I was still fuming, sitting in the front with Lena. She just sang along to the radio till we got there, stopping eventually outside a Hollywood-style metal gate perched in the middle of a stone perimeter wall with palms scratching the sky above it. It swooshed open when Lena pressed something on a black fob.

"Oooooh, look – a prancing pony!" shouted Gemma, breaking the black mood. At the left of the gate, on top of a majestic curved sandstone wall surrounded by lush bushes, cacti and mini palms, was a statue of a prancing horse, its hooves in the air. The cobbled drive sloped down to the front of the villa, and that stretched up above us, shading the car. There was a small balcony overlooking the courtyard drive and a window next to it, framed with a burnt-orange border. That was the theme throughout – white walls and orange border surrounding each window and door.

Old-fashioned Cinderella-style steps, decorated in traditional Spanish orange and blue flowery-patterned ceramic square tiles, swept up from the courtyard to the next level, which was where the dark wood front door lurked. Now *I'm* sounding like *OK Magazine*. Opposite the prancing pony was an ornamental rickety wooden cart with wagon wheels – you couldn't miss it. It was filled with bright-coloured pots, and flowers, ivy and cacti spilled out of them. Hidden behind that was a low wall with an ornate half-open black metal gate. I had a nose and found a secret garden. A large expanse of that thick, spiky Mediterranean grass rolled down to another perimeter wall that ran alongside the road we had come on. It was huge! The sun was already sunburn central at ten in the morning. I could feel my scalp itching as rays burrowed in my hair to find some pink skin to scorch.

"Come on, Lilla! We're going inside," yelled Sam. She was lugging her rucksack up the steps along with my troublesome record box. I ran to help, the heat working its magic on my frazzled nerves.

"There's a pond too. Look." Katie was pointing to the garden dipping down from the left of the steps. It was like a jungle, but organized in a chaotic sort of way. Medium-sized palms, lime-green frondy fern things, more cacti, purple flute flowers and creepers all fought for space, with the pond peeping from underneath it all, dappled with sunlight. Another statue sat on the edge of the water – a fairy or nymph – her hand reaching out to us, beckoning us in for a dip.

Lena opened the door and we trooped into the entry hall. "Bloody Nora" was the overall consensus. It was as grand as a cathedral. Well, not quite, but it was very tall, with a staircase going up to the roof. "That doesn't lead anywhere," Lena said as she saw me itching to investigate. "There's just a locked room at the top where Jules keeps stuff he wants out the way when he isn't around. He says you can go wherever you like, do what you want, just don't have too many wild parties and anything you break he wants replaced. Fag burns too, watch it." She eyed Gemma at this point. "I told him you were nice girls who wouldn't dream of getting into trouble." And she pushed her tongue firmly into her cheek.

The walls inside were all white too, and the

arched roof in the hall was held up by dark wooden beams with a grandiose chandelier hanging from the highest point – very Elton John. Immediately on the left of the hall was a bedroom and bathroom, then a corridor ran off from the right-hand wall. Straight ahead was a door that led to the kitchen, and then one just to the right that was the living-room door. "There are enough bedrooms for you to have one each."

"How coooooool! Let's go explore." Gemma led us down the corridor; we passed a bedroom, a bathroom, another bedroom and at the very end was the mother of all shagging-palace rooms. It was beautiful. A king-size double bed made of that dark wood the Spaniards love so much commanded the space: it looked like a sleigh or a boat, with curved head and foot boards. There was an old antique dressing table that went up to my chest with a carved wood mirror above it and a built-in wardrobe for all my millions of designer outfits. Daydreaming again. But best of all was a set of French doors leading out on to a big balcony that overlooked the garden and the hills beyond. I could now see the grass panned out all around the villa up to the terrace at the back, but I couldn't see what was there because there was a wall covered in purple clematis blocking off a complete view of the garden, I guessed for privacy. As you can tell, I already felt like the room was mine. . .

"This is Jules's room, all the others are guest bedrooms. Whoever sleeps in here has to be careful – the furniture is really expensive."

"I'll sleep here," I blurted out. I didn't care if anyone else wanted to, I felt the need for this room – it was so calm and cool and it had the most campest fuzzy felt picture on the wall above the bed of the Virgin Mary enveloped in light and Jules had actually wound fairy lights round the gilt frame. I loved it!

"We didn't stand a chance really, did we, with that picture on the wall." Katie smiled – she knew about my love of kitsch. Everyone else amicably chose rooms. Gemma's was the double midnight-blue room next to the bathroom. "Well, I spend ages getting ready and the bathroom *is* my fave place in the house."

"Only 'cos you end up honking your guts up after most nights out," jeered Sam.

Katie was in the pink twin room nearest mine with the mini balcony overlooking the courtyard and Sam took the yellow room just off the hallway near the kitchen with its own bathroom. I had a sneaky suspicion Gemma would have preferred her own bathroom, but she wanted a double bed more!

"Don't you want to see the pool?" asked Lena.

"I don't know if I can take any more surprises," said Sam as we trampled through the living room. And what a room it was! Time for more *OK* style pointers: *and as you sweep into the delightful living room you are instantly impressed by the split-level space with a tasteful* (read as bloody expensive) *giant farmhouse peasant-style dining table near the kitchen door.* (I wonder if any peasants ever ate at it?) *Moroccan-style rugs cover the earth-coloured floor tiles and comfy chocolate leather sofas are strewn with fluffy white cushions.* (This is obviously a place with a woman's touch, or he's gay.) *Climb the Gaudi-inspired tiled steps and you are instantly standing in a cosy TV lounge with another leather sofa, easy chairs and wide screen TV. On the distressed chunky wooden shelves* (probably made by some peasant, the same one as the table, for one Euro and flogged to tourists for a million) *various statues of the Virgin Mary sit looking pained, and other saintly artefacts take pride of place.* Actually there was a wind-up nun that spat fire, Jesus with bendy arms and a set of wheels so he could glide like the real thing and a Buddha looking like he was pulling a poo smile. There was also a candle in the shape of a painfully large willy – stylish.

We scampered out through the double doors on to the vine-covered terrace that stretched the length of the villa from the kitchen window almost to my bedroom. Vines climbing up the posts, clematis and potted plants gave it a real traditional Spanish feel. And a not so traditional disco ball hung in the centre of the ceiling. There was another table and chairs so we could eat outside.

"OHMIGOD! This place is AMAZING!" Gemma being very vocal as usual. She was right, and then, just when we thought the villa couldn't get more amazing, it did. The pool! Oh, the pool, the pool, the pool.

"It has a dolphin at the bottom." Sam was standing on the edge, mesmerized by the aquamarine water. If you went down some steps you were on the paved patio area and main garden sun terrace. The pool was in the centre – a decent size – surrounded by white sunbeds, the odd drinks table and four Coca Cola beach umbrellas (one each!). Trees and palms were everywhere all round the edge of the patio, keeping nosy parkers at bay – not that there were any other villas next to us. The nearest one was further up the hill and we could just about see it through the trees. But we did have someone checking us out — there were gnomes everywhere! All around the garden, poking out of bushes, in plant pots, spying. One of them had a well to sit by with a fishing rod and one of them was on a toadstool. Another one was dressed in drag and was smoking a cigar! "They are kind of freaky, aren't they," said Katie, picking up one that closely resembled David Beckham in a pointy red hat. Everywhere I looked a set of eyes was following me. Gemma was in hysterics.

"There's no place like gnome. . ." Sam laughed to herself.

"Yes, Jules loves his gnomes. Every time he comes out here, he brings another one from home." Lena shook her head in amusement. "Be careful with them." What did she think we were going to do, take them clubbing with us? Then again. . .

"Oh — we have a barbecue too!" squeaked Katie. She'd spotted it down the side of the villa and also found the washing line, the side door to the kitchen and yet another table and chairs under a grapevine-covered trellis. And a gnome dressed as a chef. Trumpet-shaped baby-pink flowers wafted in the breeze on the trellis. I felt like I was in paradise, invaded by gnomes. "Does he have names for them all?" Gemma giggled.

"You have a gardener and a pool boy once a week," Lena said, ignoring her. "Just so you don't freak when you see a strange man wandering around. Raul isn't interested in women, believe me," she said quickly when Gemma's eyes twinkled. "I can't speak for the pool boy. I'm going now; I have to get back for the *OK* thing."

"Thanks, Lena. It was really kind of you to help us out. We really appreciate it, don't we girls?" Everyone cooed. "I promise we'll look after the place."

"Look, here's my mobile number. Call any time." She looked like she wanted to say something else. "Please come and see your dad while you're here, Philippa. Can we forget the row this morning? He just worries, I can tell – you're still his little girl."

I shuffled in my flip-flops. "Whatever." I had NEVER been Dad's little girl.

She let my snotty reply go. "Remember too, if you want to come to Nectar any time, let me know and you'll get VIP passes. Your dad plays there every Friday and Saturday. Any other nights are pretty easy for me to get you into as well; us promoters know one another. Don't pay for entry, you haven't got the money!"

"Thanks." That was nice of her. She was probably trying to butter me up.

"Bye girls. Have fun."

Katie gripped my hand. "Are you OK? Your dad was pretty mad this morning."

"I'm fine, honestly. I knew he'd be like that if he found out I was into DJing – that's why I've never told him. He's being a typical bloke and expecting me not have a clue 'cos I'm a girl." I shrugged. "I'm sorry we had a row, it must have been embarrassing."

"Naaah. Don't worry. I know what your dad's like!" She smiled and changed the subject. "I am so glad I came. This villa is perfect. I had no idea it was going to be so chilled. I'm really looking forward to my birthday now." EEEEK! I had completely forgotten to tell the others Katie was going to be eighteen tomorrow.

Thank God we weren't staying at Dad's after today's debacle. This place was so much better and we were on our own – we could have a proper breakfast party for Katie now and not have to worry about getting told off! All we needed was some music. . .

There was evidence every now and then that a DJ lived here. Piles of *DJ* magazine in the loo, black and white photos on the wall in the hall and living room of Jules playing at Homelands, him with more famous DJs, a pic of him with my dad (!) with the Space logo behind them. Dad looked wasted – he was gooning for the camera wearing his best Steve Wheeler "I am a mentalist" face. What I was really hoping to find wasn't here, though: a set of decks and a banging sound system. He wouldn't bring them with him each time 'cos he would be jetting back and forwards the whole summer. . .

"The air smells so sweet. I want to walk around naked," said Sam, as she ran to the gate leading to steps down to the other bit of grassy garden.

"What are we waiting for? Let's have a pool party, NNNNOOOOOW!" And Gemma jumped in in her micro-shorts and bikini top, sunglasses and flip-flops. "Throw me a gnome – I may as well practise my pulling powers on someone."

chapter
five

"I think we need a set of wheels if we're going to get about," Sam said, as we checked out what was in the kitchen and the tiny store room right between Sam's bathroom and the kitchen where all the pots and pans were stacked precariously on shelves. The room was big and square with a window hatch by the sink so we could pass stuff out into the garden when eating outside. The fridge was like something from Star Trek – all chrome with an ice-maker and water fountain in the door. "We need some food and drink to put in this . . . thing. Do you know how to get into town?"

"There's a place in Jesus that hires out mopeds. I'm starving, so we should go now!"

"Who's going to ride the mopeds? I've never ridden one before," asked Katie nervously as we left the villa through the main gate, swooshing it closed behind us. It was like something from the Hollywood Hills.

"Well, I can drive and so can Sam, so I guess we just blag it and show our driving licences," I replied, determined not to let Doubting Thomas make me change my mind. Every now and then there would be a waft of something heavenly, almost like burnt sugar, blown gently through the air. Cacti, olive trees and fig trees lined the dirt road that morphed into tarmac as we headed away from the small cluster of villas set into the hillside. The sun was really caning it now. Heat rose up from the ground as we walked down the slope, making the end of the road disappear in a silvery haze. I half expected to see Lawrence of Arabia on his camel shimmer into view. The sky was a searing baby blue at the edges and the higher up you looked, the more saturated it became. I could see a crescent moon really faint, stuck on like fuzzy felt. A couple of cars passed us, one or two slowed so they could take a better look. I'm sure it was more to do with Gemma's sequinned shorts, or lack of them.

"Gem, are those shorts appropriate for shopping and riding a moped?" Sam quizzed her. We were all wearing combat shorts and vest tops.

"But it's Ibiza. I thought we were supposed to be dressed like this all the time!" she said indignantly, picking them out of her crack.

"If you want to get propositioned, maybe. I'm not sure the Super Mercado can cope with your arse hanging out of that Band Aid." Those two were off again; they were like a married couple.

We eventually made it into Jesus, picking our way carefully along the busy dual carriageway. It got a bit hairy as lorries thundered by, not caring if they squashed us or not. After about five minutes, though, the road reduced back down to one lane and we recognized the garage on the corner and then the rest of the strip came into view. I spotted the moped hire place – it was a car rental shop in the modern arcade of shops that also housed the supermarket. I was the only one who could speak any Spanish, and even that was pitiful schoolgirl level.

"*Buenos tardes. Puedo acquiar un moto, por favor?*"

"Of course," the guy replied in perfect English. Why bother trying?

We had to fill in forms, signing our lives away. Lordy knows what would happen if we had an accident. . .

"Have you ridden these before, ladies?"

He took us through the gear changes, and I had to ride round the car park at the back. It wasn't too bad until I stalled it and nearly went flying into a skip full of broken glass and wood.

"Fucking hell, Lilla. Are you sure you can do this?" asked Gemma. Meaning, the promise of a snog with a minor soap star couldn't persuade me to get on the back with you. I had to have a practice with Katie on it.

"Lilla, I'm really not sure about this. Mum would have a fit if she knew we were on bikes. So many people get killed every year on them, especially here, with all the drugs and stuff." Here we go. I knew she was going to be like this, she had been quiet all the way down to the village.

"Well, how are we going to get around? You

have to be over twenty-one to hire a car. It's not like we've a lot of money, and we can't take taxis each time we want to go to the beach. I'm not staying in the villa every day for a month — Ibiza's so beautiful, we should make the most of it."

"I know, but we wouldn't do this at home, be so reckless." Oooh, Katie — uptight Prissy Miss. . . I could see Gemma and Sam rolling their eyes.

"No, we wouldn't, that's why we came on holiday. Trust me — if you feel unsafe and want to get off, I'll stop. Just give it a chance."

So she did.

Half an hour later, we were on our way to Ibiza Old Town for some lunch and a nose round. I had Katie on the back and was in front of Sam 'cos I sort of knew the way. I could hear her buzzing behind me like a hairdryer on acid. We all looked like we had pool balls on our heads. "I'd rather risk brain damage than wear this thing," Gemma had moaned when the helmet was forced upon her. Fashion victim first, RTA victim second.

The moped was dead easy to ride once you got the hang of changing gear. We were creaming along in fourth, sunglasses on to keep the bugs out, Katie was clenching me round my middle, almost cutting off my air supply, but so far hadn't asked me to stop. I negotiated the roundabouts OK, only once going round twice 'cos I got a bit lost. Soon we were cruising down the typical windy Mediterranean streets of the town, checking out funky shops and making mental notes of places we wanted to see again. I swerved into a space reserved for bikes one street behind the marina and we dismounted.

Katie was white. "Are you OK?" I asked, taking off my helmet.

"Hmmm . . . yes. Those lorries get a bit close, don't they?" was all she said. I could tell she was trying to be brave and not be a party-pooper. Bless.

"Ooooooh, look at all the clothes shops . . . and the men!" Yes, you could hardly miss the men. Everyone was so hubba hubba, and dressed in expensive-looking clothes, even if they weren't the height of fashion. We turned down a side street and were welcomed by the sea twinkling at the end. On either side of us were little shops selling beach mats, lilos, rubber rings, postcards, cigarettes, etc, etc. And every so often there was the odd bar stuck in the middle of this wall of incongruous merchandise. I forget that people actually come here to go to the beach with their kids, not to take Es, dance like loons and stay up for three days without going to bed.

I gave the girls a whirlwind tour of the town. We skirted round the marina and all the hip bars and restaurants, and Dalt Villa – the impressive walled part of the city on the very top of the hill, housing the castle and the cathedral perched on the toppermost poppermost bit of the hill. Gemma was only interested in the dinky boutiques and jewellery shops – oh, and smiling at boys – while Sam wanted to know where the best clubs were for underground house music and undiscovered DJs. Katie just breezed along looking at the Moorish architecture and pointing out "interesting" facts from the guidebook. "Did you know that the city used to be invaded by pirates in the sixteenth century, that's why they built the wall?"

"Pity they can't build another one to keep the England shirts out," Sam sneered. I thought it seemed to be working 'cos I'd only spotted about two since we'd arrived.

Lunch was a laid-back affair on the marina, dazzled by sun bouncing off the sea and entertained by seagulls stealing food from passing tourists. The smell of fried garlic mingling with the salty fresh sea air fanned our appetite. Sam chose a tapas bar with the best tables outside on the sea front. "We have to try the local food, I'm *not* going to Maccy D's!" Dizzy with choice we ordered a feast of garlic-butter prawns, *patatas bravas*, Spanish tortilla, marinated anchovies, Serrano ham, octopus in chilli sauce and tantalizing saffron-laced paella. "Here's to the best holiday we'll ever have, for the next five years, at least!" Gemma toasted with the red wine poured from a clay carafe. We clinked tumblers, the Four Musketeers, our first real day together in Ibiza, gorging our faces on flavours that couldn't be recreated at home, because how could you contrive the unique spice of Ibizan life?

Stuffed beyond belief and sleepy (not good when riding mopeds) we whipped up clouds of dust back towards the villa. We really needed to stock up on supplies; we didn't even have any beer – disaster! As we reached Jesus we pulled into the lay-by next to the supermarket. I was getting the hang of this moped thing. The lorries were a worry, but if you held on tight and didn't breathe, it was OK, sort of.

"I think we should have a kitty for food, drink and petrol," Sam said as she unclipped her attractive blue helmet. She made everyone cough up the readies before we ventured into the local shop. Katie was in front getting a trolley so I took the opportunity to tell Sam and Gem about her birthday tomorrow. "I thought we could get champagne and a cake and then go out in the evening. I know a really cool place called Souk, she'll love it."

The supermarket was ace. They must have been used to fussy stars asking for marinated tofu and reduced-fat bananas. It was more like a deli. We skidded up and down the aisles like we were on *Supermarket Sweep*, grabbing stuff, throwing it in the trolley: bulbous sun-ripened tomatoes still on the vine, sun-blushed black cherries, Serrano ham (five packs!), blocks of cheese, crusty loaves, a mountain of tinned toms, rice and pasta and the rest. Plus myriad bottles of booze – everything you could imagine for cocktails. Gemma and Katie had to get a taxi back with it all.

After we'd unloaded the shopping, Gemma and Katie sloped off outside to fry in the sun. Sam and I chatted at the table outside underneath the vines, sipping cool beers from the fridge. I was feeling restless. "This place belongs to a DJ, so how come there're no decks?"

"I know what you mean. I was looking for his CD player earlier – nothing." Sam was like me, a real freak about music. Her dream was to be a music journalist – she had a place at journalism college in London, pending A level results. She wanted to write about it, while I wanted to play it.

"Are you thinking what I'm thinking?" And I cocked my head inside and up.

"The top of the stairs!" we both said at the same time.

chapter

six

"There must be a key somewhere." Sam was rattling the doorknob. There was no landing, just the top step and this midget-sized, solid wood door. It was like something from *Alice in Wonderland*.

"I saw some keys on hooks in the kitchen." So I bolted down the stairs and grabbed the selection hanging up by the back door.

"None of them work – look, they're all the wrong size." Sam handed them back. "They must be spares for the French doors and back door. If we can find a thick piece of plastic, longer than a credit card, I might be able to do it that way."

We went back down and looked in drawers in the living room, the kitchen and all the bedrooms. "If only we had a record or something – that would do it," Sam sighed.

"But we do! I have my tunes here. They're in my room!" I legged it there and riffled through the box, pulling up one after another, trying to choose one that I wouldn't be too heartbroken about if we broke or scratched it. It was a hard decision! I eventually found one I knew I had on another twelve-inch at home. Sam was very impressed. She understood about the preciousness of records.

She slid it down the side of the door where the lock connected with the frame. "How do you know what to do?" I asked.

"I saw it in a film. . . I think I have to press back against the lock, like this." And as she did it, the door opened slightly with a Hammer Horror creak, making us both jump.

"Sam – you genius." She pushed it open and a wall of heat hit us. A very small window overlooking the pool opposite let in some light through the grubby film coating it. Everything was bathed in a grey winter-morning half-light, and Sam and I could pick out old garden furniture, boxes and shapes covered in sheets. It was very cobwebby and the ceiling was really low, which made sense 'cos the roof was flat. Only a dwarf could have stood up in it. Or a gnome. . .

"Do you think we can walk on the floor? What if we fall through?"

Sam got on her hands and knees and pressed the floor. "It's floorboards, we should be OK."

She stood up, half crouching and I followed her in. It smelled of dust and I could feel a sneeze building up. We shuffled through the boxes, jumping every time a floorboard sounded like it was going to give way. I saw something I recognized.

"Sam — a record box!" She stood up and banged her head. Over to the right there was what looked like a table with a what-used-to-be-white cloth covering two oblong shapes. Could it be? I climbed over what looked like an old diving board. The removal of the cloth stirred up a year's-worth of dust and the sneeze that had been hovering exploded — when I opened my eyes, there, as if by magic, were two deck flight cases and a box with a mixer in it. "Bingo!" The effort had made me sweat like I was on death row.

"They're no good to us if we haven't got speakers and an amp though, are they?" She looked around, hoping to spot them. It was a bit like finding a pair of Gucci trousers at a jumble sale, getting them home and then realizing they didn't fit or even look that nice. What a bummer.

"Keep looking, he'll have put them up here with the decks to keep them safe." We looked in every box, under every sheet, until I found a large Bang & Olufsen cardboard box by the window. In it was the sound system with an amp, CD player and four small speakers, the kind that can twist metal girders they're so loud.

"Now the holiday can really begin," said Sam, looking as pleased as me. "We'd better be careful with all this; we'll be dog food if he finds out we broke into the secret hiding place."

An hour later, while Gemma and Katie had been baking like burgers on a barbecue, we had humped all the gear downstairs and set up the decks near the French doors on the table that we'd moved from near the kitchen.

"Go get your records and let's have some fun.

I haven't heard you play yet." As I skidded back to my room to grab the wax and headphones, I had a feeling of dainty little elephants trampling through my guts. What if I was shit? What if Sam just laughed and said I was wasting my time? Katie had heard me play when I was really shite, but to be honest, she didn't really have a clue.

I started with an old favourite just to test the levels, making sure it wasn't too loud and that I could work out how to use the mixer (which was like a flight deck – flashing lights, sliders, loads of channels and a multitude of knobs) then I got stuck in. Sam placed a beer next to me and sat down halfway in the villa and halfway out. I found the next record I wanted to play and put it on the other turntable – now I was lost, I wasn't in Ibiza, I could have been anywhere, all I had to do was bring in the next tune. The key to mixing is finding a point where the tune playing would totally benefit from the second tune just coming in, blending, mixing in, making the first tune better, funking it up so that the beats are like two hearts pressed against each other, matching beat for beat, so they become one sound. I did it and it sounded good to me, I played around with the EQs, dropping the bass from the first tune and bringing the incoming tune right in, so that now it dominated the living room. I bent down to get the next record and when I stood up, there were Gemma, Katie and Sam, staring at me, open-mouthed. Sam motioned me to take my head-phones off – I couldn't hear anything apart from the new tune.

"Bloody hell, Lilla. That was amazing. Like, you don't know how amazing that was. I had no idea that you were *that* good." She came round to my side of the decks and gave me the biggest hug. "You have to do something with this, now, while we're here."

"Yes – Lilla, shit, I mean, you were cool as fuck. I mean, you could be like, the next Lottie, no, you're better than her," Gemma said before I could protest.

"Wow," Katie gasped. "You look like you know what you're doing. What I just heard was pretty amazing – you blended it seamlessly. I didn't know where one record ended and one began. You sounded just like one of the Ibiza mix CDs." Coming from Katie, I knew she meant that as a compliment.

"Lilla, please, I think you should try and get a gig somewhere while we're here. Lena could help, or your dad," Sam went on.

"NO WAY! I'm not having Dad or Lena pulling any strings. I want to get somewhere on my own, no help required, not after his shitty comments this morning. He'd just think I was crap anyway!" I snapped back.

"OK, don't throw all your toys out the pram. I was only saying." Sam looked miffed.

"Can we just forget it. Do you want to hear some tunes or not?" And I slammed on my headphones and whacked up the volume. End of convo. I wasn't even sure if I wanted to take this anywhere. I mean, who would want to pay to see *me* play? I'm not even famous. . .

It was early evening and I had been playing for about half an hour. Gemma, quite pissed, was clutching a beer and dancing on the sofa in her black string bikini with diamonds studded all over it. "We need to find some boys so we can have a proper party," she shouted above the music. Katie was blissed out on a sun-lounger by the pool drinking some bright pink drink and reading a girlie magazine, her feet tapping in time with the bass. Sam was going through my records and choosing what I had to put on next and making sure I had enough beer – she was my DJ bitch.

Chilling was the name of the game. Katie's birthday was in the morning and we didn't all want to be talking to God on the big white telephone. It looked like Gemma might be, though. . .

"What was that?" Gemma shouted above the music, stopping her pole-dancing routine without the pole. "I thought I heard someone at the door." I turned down the volume and sure enough, there was banging on the front door.

"How did they get to the door without opening the gate?" Sam asked, sounding worried.

"Come on, let's go see," Gemma slurred to Sam. Katie had come in to see what we were talking about. We heard the door open and a man's voice shouted.

"Jules? You old queen. You didn't tell me you'd arrived." And into the living room charged one of the most beautiful men I had ever seen — cheekbones I could have hung off, wide-set green eyes, trendy fluffy-spiky dark-brown bed-hair and the most toned body ever. He stood there in combat shorts and white vest that clung to his ripples, looking round the room. I heard Katie's sharp intake of breath. She too was caught with her tongue out. God did exist.

"I just heard Jules on the decks – where's he hiding? JULES?" He looked out to the pool. His accent was Scottish, and slightly camp. Doh! God worked in mysterious ways. . .

"Jules isn't here. Who are you?" I said, feeling disappointed as there was every chance he didn't bat for our team.

"Sorry, darling, where are my manners! I'm Andy."

Gemma and Sam stood behind him – Gemma was making signs of fainting and phwoarr faces. I don't think the penny'd dropped with her. "*I'm* Gemma," she gushed, "and this is Sam, Katie and Lilla."

"Darlings, where are you hiding Jules?" he asked all of us.

"We're not hiding him anywhere. We're looking after this place for him while he gets better." Katie answered, batting her eyelashes. Not her as well!

"What d'you mean? *Gets better?*" So I filled him in about the car accident and how Jules was out of action for the rest of the summer. He would get better, but not enough to be back at work for ages.

"Poor Jules. No wonder he didn't call to let me

know he'd arrived." He then seemed to notice that I was behind the decks with headphones round my neck and the volume turned right down. "So, it was *you* I heard DJing?"

"Err, yeah."

"You were great. I thought it was Jules. So, are you taking his place at Nectar and Space?"

I laughed. "Me? No, no, I was just messing about on his decks."

"Darling, that was no messing!"

I could see Gemma looking like a huff was about to descend on her. She was always used to being centre of attention where men were concerned. Not with this one.

"That's what *I've* been telling her," said Sam and looked at me as if to say, "Told you so."

"Well, you know what this means, don't you?" Andy said. We all shook our heads. "It means, Girlfriend, get on those decks and spin us some tunes." Sam winked, she guessed he wasn't on our bus, but Gemma was still clueless. This could be hilarious.

"I'll get the drinks, what are we having?" and Gemma took orders and disappeared off into the kitchen where glasses started clinking.

"I think we are going to feel shit tomorrow,"

whispered Katie, biting her lip as I put another tune on the decks and turned the volume up.

"Yep. But that's the whole idea of Ibiza, if you don't feel chod at least once, then you didn't have a good time." Bring it oooooon. . .

chapter
seven

It was four in the morning and I had to go to bed. My mouth felt like Gandhi's flip-flop. Gemma was passed out on a sunbed, sunnies on, topless, in just her diamond bikini bottoms. She had a fag stub in hand, a ring of ash underneath her on the patio. Her mouth was open – anything could have fallen in there. Katie was already in bed – she pooped early – and Sam was slumped at the table outside looking over the pool, drinking a cranberry juice and desperately trying to stave off a hangover.

I stood at the edge of the pool, wondering if a dip would sober me up or make me chunder.

I'd switched the music off half an hour ago after I'd played the same tunes twice already. Andy had disappeared about half an hour earlier, apologizing about the state of the place, but it wasn't too bad, just glasses and beer bottles dotted here and there, and ashtrays full to the brim on the table outside. Now I could hear the real nightlife in the hills – the crickets buzzing, a soothing symphony that would hopefully help me sleep.

The gnomes were obviously mortified at our lewd behaviour – Andy had turned their backs so they didn't have to witness it. I blushed when I recalled the naked pool antics – Gemma had thrown Katie in after she'd laughed at Gemma's pulling techniques falling flat. Then we all jumped in and a very drunk Andy ordered clothes off. Gemma willingly obliged while Katie scarpered. That left me (pants on), Sam (pants on), Gemma (you can guess) and naked Andy in the pool (nnnngggnnn, I can't speak, it's up there with my biggest fantasy: headlining at the Ministry of Sound).

"I cannot believe our luck, Andy living just up the hill and being a dancer at Pacha." The movie of our holiday was hotting up. Not only had we made friends with one of the sexiest men alive (admittedly, he was gay, but it could just be a phase . . . please, God), he was also a mover and shaker, inviting us to his nights on VIP passes so we could see him dance.

"The look on Gemma's face when she realized he was gay – she looked like she'd lost a winning Lotto ticket," Sam giggled. Gemma had been flirting so hard, knocking back drinks and forcing Andy to keep up with her on her quest for oblivion. Thank God we weren't out in a club 'cos I would have battered her over the head to calm her down – she was really out of control, and I could tell she was freaking Katie out with her over the top behaviour. She'd tried to stay naked after we all got out of the pool, dancing on a drinks table. Sam went mental and dragged her inside to put on her bikini bottoms 'cos that's all she would agree to wear.

Sam rubbed her eyes, making them more red than they were before. "We're going to be rough as old dogs tomorrow – we never ate any dinner *and* we still haven't hung the banner for Katie."

"I'll get it. D'you think we should wake her?" I asked gesturing to coma girl on the sunbed.

"Naah. Just throw a towel on her, she'll be fine. I don't think I can cope with one of her drunken rants. I'm making cheese on toast, want some?"

I heard someone pottering in the kitchen at about five am when I went for a wee. Just as I flushed, there was an almighty crash, then silence. Gemma! Katie was ahead of me, rubbing her eyes and flicking switches. The light was on in the kitchen but no one was in there. The kettle was boiling furiously and toast was burning under the grill. Katie ran forward to pull it out from underneath with an oven glove and I took the kettle off the hob. "Where is she?" Katie coughed, wafting the smoke around. Sam wandered in looking green and opened the back door to let in some air. Gemma wasn't in the living room.

"Hang on, the store-room door's open," Katie said. We hadn't noticed 'cos we'd come in through the living room. Sam switched the light on and there, underneath a pile of pans, was Gemma, bikini bottoms round her ankles, flat on her back covered in baking trays and cake tins. "Gemma – shit – are you OK?" Katie bent down and started pulling the trays and tins off her.

Gemma let out a groan. "Where's the loo

gone?" she said still lying on her back. As Katie cleared the tins, we noticed Gemma had weed all over the floor! Sam pulled her pants up for her.

"Oh, Gemma – why do you always get in this state?" Sam lamented. "Here, Lils, can you grab her other arm and we'll pull her up?"

She was a dead weight, but we managed to peel her off the floor. "Let's put her in bed." So we dragged/carried her to her room and laid her on top of the covers. She looked white.

"Where am I?" she asked in a weak voice.

"In bed," Sam said. "Can you remember what happened?"

"No. I feel sick."

"Katie – can you grab a pan or a bucket?" I shouted.

She ran in with a wok just as Gemma sat up and sprayed red wine into it. Katie caught it like a tennis player!

When Gemma'd finished she just lay back down without a word and fell asleep straight away.

"I'll sleep in here with her," Sam offered. "She might need me in the middle of the night."

"She must have pulled the tins down on top of her when she realized the loo wasn't there," Katie guessed.

It was almost light outside and I was knackered. Katie emptied the wok and put it back by the bed. We left Sam as nurse – it was a job she was used to by now, being Gemma's best friend. . .

chapter
eight

I made sure everyone was awake before Katie by setting the alarm on my phone. It had been hard getting Gemma out of bed and she looked like death, but she managed it, walking like she was treading on eggshells. She didn't remember a thing about weeing on the floor and surprisingly hadn't been sick again. Sam had managed to get some sleep after all. "Have you got the champagne ready?" Gemma asked when she shuffled outside.

"We bloody need it more than her, hair of the dog and all that."

"Ooooh, someone got a hangover?" I laughed, amazed Gemma wasn't embarrassed about the whole weeing thing.

"No, I must have had a dodgy beer. Course I've got a hangover, haven't you?"

"Not too bad, Sam and I sobered up while *we* did the tidying."

"Shhhhh! I can hear her coming out here." We were all standing by the table on the veranda. It must have been about ten am – the sun was its usual perky self, showering us grateful serfs with its glorious rays. Katie wandered through the living room yawning, wearing her knickers and an old school hockey T-shirt. When she hit the French doors, we frightened her to death: "Happy Birthday!!!!"

"Argh! OHMIGOD!" She was staring open-mouthed at the table, hands either side of her head. We had been busy. Slices of melon wrapped in Serrano ham were all fanned out on a bright green ceramic platter. A pile of presents lay invitingly at one end, Gemma popped the cork on a bottle of champers – we even had real champagne flutes (I'd expect nothing less from our party boy, Jules). In the middle of the table stood the almond cake from the supermarket, looking far more attractive now I had put the candles on it and lit them. Warm buttery croissants and some swirly bun things with cinnamon and raisins perched in a breadbasket. Sam had scooted off on the moped early this morning and treated us to a special breakfast from the café in Jesus. Best of all was a banner declaring "Happy Eighteenth Birthday" strung up on vines behind our heads, with balloons randomly tied to branches and chairs. I had commandeered a few of the gnomes to look like they were at a party on the table and window ledge — each had a party popper tied round its hand and streamers strewn on its head. "Ohhhh, thank you, thank you. I love the gnomes." And she came over and gave us a big hug.

"Have some champagne — it'll wake you up." Gemma proffered a glass of ice-cold pale gold bubbles.

"Just what I need." We all clinked glasses and sipped the morning luxury. "Here's to more mornings like this on holiday. Can I blow out the candles?"

"Yes, then you have to open your presents."

And as she took a deep breath we all sang Happy Birthday. We sat at the table while she ripped paper and envelopes.

Gemma screeched when she saw what Katie'd got from her mum and dad. "A Tiffany coffee-bean necklace – I have wanted one of those, like, for ever. You lucky cow!" It was so understated, three silver coffee beans strung together on a silver chain – very pop star. Her brother Ant had given her Mac Lip Glass and some glitter – essential for any Ibiza babe – and my present was a pair of J-Lo pink towelling "ho" hot pants and a pair of matching pink glittery flip-flops. "Ohh, Lils, thanks – I love them. Can I wear these out clubbing, or will they be a bit much?"

"Yes, wear them," Gemma said before I could say they were just meant for the beach; Katie would never normally wear stuff like that out. "I have a pair exactly the same in baby blue."

As we were tucking in for the celebratory breakfast, Katie's moby went. It was her mum. It was relentless for about half an hour as friends from school and aunties and uncles wished her happy birthday. Just as she was sipping the second glass of champagne, the phone went again. She went quiet when she saw who it was.

"It's Tom."

"Don't answer it," Sam said.

"He'll just keep ringing if I don't."

"Let him. Switch it off."

She let it ring off, and then it started ringing again. After the third try, she huffed and answered, walking over to the pool. "He sounds like a real wanker," said Sam in a low voice. "She was telling me about him last night."

"Oh, he is. And he's a control freak too. He used to make snidey comments if she wore really sexy clothes out with the girls from school, just to a party or something. She became really self-conscious about what she wore and how she is."

"Thing is, I don't think she's convinced herself it's over," Sam continued. "She wants to have a good time and loosen up. I was watching her last night, it was like she wished she could have taken her clothes off in the pool, but something was stopping her."

"That's 'cos Tom makes her think she can't have a good time without him. It's soooo ridiculous. This could really help her, being with just girls and not having to think about if she's *allowed* all the time."

Katie was sitting with her legs in the pool. I could see she was getting upset. "Leave her." Sam held on to my arm as I went to go and grab the phone. "She has to sort this herself."

She switched it off and came back to the table with watery eyes. "He won't leave me alone. He keeps going on about when I get back, how he'll meet me at the airport. Why don't I come home now so we can sort this all out before we go to med school together." Then she burst into tears properly. "I miss him. . ." Jeeeeeeeeez!

I rubbed her back and made the usual soothing noises while Sam refilled her champagne flute. "You've done the right thing. Now come on, it's your birthday, you're not allowed to cry, it's against the Geneva Convention." That raised a smile.

"You're not going to the same Uni? Are you mad?" Gemma, tactful as ever.

"Only if he gets the grades on his retakes." Katie blew her nose on a piece of kitchen towel. "I thought it was a good idea at the time, it meant I would know someone there."

"Yes, but it's also the kiss of death to having a good time. The whole point is to meet new people. My sister's friend, Janine, went to the same

Uni as her school boyfriend and she never made any friends 'cos she hung out with him all the time. Then he dumped her at the end of the second year and she hardly knew anyone. Imagine that?" We did and it sounded heinous. Katie never listened to me when *I* said that.

"Yes, but it wasn't going to be like that." She looked dangerously close to snivelling again.

"But it sounds like *he* wants it like that. He doesn't like you being here on a girlie holiday and you're not even going out with him any more, are you?" Gemma was getting away with stuff I was never allowed to say.

"I don't know what to do – he was really upset. Saying he missed me and that he thought about me every day. I wish I could see him." A tear ran down her face and she hastily wiped it. We pretended not to notice.

"Don't even go there. He fucked up. It's over, end of story. You might meet someone else out here. We have a whole month to see what happens. Get used to being single again." Gemma was rubbing her hands together in glee at the thought of all those boys out there, just waiting for her.

"But I couldn't. I've only ever, you know, done it, with Tom."

Uh-oh. Sex Talk. This was one thing Katie knew a lot more about than me. I know we are all supposed to be swapping gossip about willies all the time, but all my stories are really boring. But I'm quite happy to hear about other people!

"Oooooh. Was he any good?"

Katie looked like she wasn't going to let on. "Yes, he was." And she blushed, sipping champagne furiously. The bubbles must have made her brave 'cos she never mentioned Tom to me, but then, she sort of knew I wasn't interested. The thought of him, all sweaty and red and ergh! NO thanks.

Gemma nodded in a scholarly way, understanding completely.

"Is this the bit where we all declare we're actually still virgins and haven't got a clue?" laughed Sam.

"Yes, well. What have you got to offer in the way of stories? Come on." Gemma challenged.

"I think that's my business," Sam answered primly.

"Only 'cos you've probably had about ten men – you're a dark horse, Samantha Bailey." Sam blushed – Gemma was probably right. Sam didn't talk about boys much, whenever we asked her about guys on the scene, she just shrugged and said they were a distraction. Gemma said it was 'cos her mum got preggers so young and had to give up any chance of a career as a photographer. Sam is scared of the same thing happening to her, I guess. Not getting pregnant, but some boy coming in and sweeping her off her feet and tying her down. "I'll neither confirm or deny reports that I'm a slapper. You'll just have to use your imagination."

"And Lilla? We know *you're* a lesbian." Gemma had given up asking about me and boys, said I was too fussy. But I hadn't given up hope of meeting a *real* man. I'd had a bit of a thing with one of the spotty Ryedale boys, Dan Millar, but it turned out that he was my dad's biggest fan and only wanted to go out with me 'cos of him. What a knob!

"Ha ha, Gemma. Do something useful and open another bottle of pop. I think today should be all about excess."

"But Lils, didn't we do that yesterday?" Katie asked all concerned.

"That was a dry run. You ain't seen nothing yet, has she girls?"

"NNNNOOOOOOO!"

Katie didn't know whether to run to the hills or start snorting vodka off a teaspoon. "Errr, OK, show me how it's done." That's my girl. . .

chapter
nine

"Come on, the taxi's here!" I rounded up the troops in the courtyard. As usual, we were waiting for Gemma to finish trowelling on her lippy. We'd spent the rest of the day just being slugs by the pool and finishing off the champagne. Sam fell asleep in the sun and had a red stripe down one side of her boobs and red ears.

At about nine pm the sun set in the hills to the right of the villa. I slid on a chill-out CD and we all sat on the veranda as the shadows crept across the patio, sinking the garden into that underwater light. The sunset was spectacular – a solid burning orb of salmon-pink and orange – and very quick as the day fizzled out and introduced a daredevil Ibiza night, our first proper escapade outside the villa. We toasted the beginning of the evening with a Margarita each, made by Sam using one of Jules's books, complete with umbrellas and salty-rimmed glass – you can always count on a gay man for the finishing touches.

"Am I wearing the right clothes?" asked Katie, dressed in a tight black pair of pinstripe hipsters and red slash-neck, cap-sleeved T. I was wearing my old faves: Miss Sixty jeans with flares you could whip up a whirlwind in, my tan already showing against my white lace-trimmed vest top. Gemma was in an electric-blue boob tube and tight jeans – she could have worn a Tesco bag and still been stunning, while Sam chose a denim mini to show off her Bambi legs and an old skool tight T with sixty-nine emblazoned on the front. Her cowboy boots were *la pièce de resistance*, however, patchwork pink-and-brown leather. She looked hot (not just her ears). We all did – babes on the loose.

"You look fab, doll. The thing with Ibiza, Katie,

is that anything goes. If you wanted to wear nipple tassels and a nurse's outfit, that would be cool too. Don't sweat it," I told her. We were on our way to Souk to have a blowout for Katie's birthday. It was a very trendy restaurant-cum-bar just outside Ibiza Town – not an experience we would be able to afford at the end of the trip 'cos it cost a wedge. But you have to experience this place – it's L'Oreal.

"It said in the guidebook that Souk used to be a brothel," Sam informed us on arrival. "They also have DJs on later in the evening and it turns into a club, sort of."

We walked through an art gallery ("modern" art – white canvases! Purlease. . .) to get to the outside restaurant with a bamboo fence shielding it from the bars further down the steps in the vast expanse of garden. We could see that it was quite busy already.

"How cool?" Katie was impressed.

By the entrance to the restaurant was a little maitre'd podium. "Do you have a table for four?" I asked the good-looking guy in my best Spanish.

He checked the bookings. "Give me fifteen minutes – grab a table in the bar and I'll come and find you."

We headed for the garden, down some stone steps, through palm trees, and came to a covered circular bar underneath a giant white Bedouin tent that stretched about fifty metres across, home to all sorts of sofas, floor cushions, fairy lights, candles, Moroccan wall hangings and those gorgeous chunky teak knee-high tables. Leading off from that tent was a whole other area at the back of the garden, accessible if you crossed a bamboo bridge. There was a dance floor that was half covered by another canopy and to the right of that a raised platform that had more sofas positioned round tables. The DJ booth was at the very back and they were spinning ambient funky house, just funky enough to get a vibe wafting through the place.

"This place is bliss," sighed Sam as she sank back on to one of the embroidered floor cushions.

"Shall I get some drinks?" offered Katie.

"I'll help." And Gemma went with her to the circular bar. Probably because the barman was like an extra from *Gladiator*. Were there no ugly people in Ibiza?

The restaurant was outside under a movie-set sky, with those oil torches burning round the perimeter to give extra light. The floor was strewn with tiny pebbles and our table was on top of rush matting. It was packed now, about twenty white-tableclothed tables arranged in the space full of people, all stylish. A lot of older men with pretty girls, though. Playboys. Some of the girls didn't look much older than us. Yuk.

We'd been sat down for about a second when a table of men to our right, all in their late thirties or forties (I can never tell, they looked older than Dad) asked a waiter to come to their table. "Those gentlemen would like to buy you young ladies a drink," he said as he handed us our menus.

"Tell them no thank you," said Sam, before anyone could say anything.

"Saaaaam! Why did you do that?" Gemma moaned.

"Look at them. They're old enough to be our dads and they're minging. Do you really want to be saddled with them for the rest of the night?" she hissed.

"But free drink!"

"Gemma! It would be weird and look at how creepy those other girls and their playboys look." I was loath to turn away a free drink, but we weren't desperate.

But the olds wouldn't be spurned without a

fight. One of them, in a P Diddy-style Versace shirt, came over and stood by Gemma. He had a very attractive shiny red forehead where the hair was obviously abandoning ship. "I believe you young ladies don't want a drink, but what if I told you it was Krug champagne? It's my good friend Jerry's birthday, you see." The least minging of the group waved and smiled, like a snake. The others were laughing like drains.

"Did you want us to lap-dance for you, or something?" asked Gemma, deadpan innocent.

He started to look uncomfortable. "No, just join us for a drink."

"I don't think our dads would be too pleased with us hanging out with guys older than them," Sam replied, smiling innocently and studying her menu like it was *War and Peace*. Gem and I smiled nicely at him; Katie hid behind her menu, going red.

You could have fried an egg on his face. He tried to laugh but looked like it was going to choke him. "Very well. Have a good evening." And off he sloped, back to his jeering mates. What a loser. I bet they were all married as well.

"Has he gone?" whispered Katie, not daring to look.

"Yes, let's order – I'm starving!" Sam clapped her hands.

The food was like something you only read about in *Vogue* magazine. Seared tuna steaks with green salsa, rocket salad, braised lamb shank with puy lentils and bruised roasted garlic cloves, herb-crusted roast breast of organic chicken, seafood ravioli in sage butter sauce – we had some difficult choices, huh? Made a change from Maccy D's. And it wasn't as expensive as I had originally thought. As we were so busy stuffing our faces, we didn't notice a table fill up just to the left. I only realized someone was there when they spoke to Sam who was sat on the end nearest to their table.

"Excuse me, is the ravioli as delicious as it looks? I'm having trouble choosing."

She looked up and her eyes widened. He was gorgeous, black, with the softest northern accent ever. "Errr, yes, it's delicious," she mumbled. That was the first time I had ever seen Sam go red when asked a question, and it was only about ravioli.

"Thank you." And he winked, not in an "Aren't I the cutest guy" way, but in a "I don't care about the ravioli and you know it" way.

Gemma nudged her. "Hubba hubba."

"He was all right."

"Are you mad, have you lost the use of your eyes?" she hissed, as they were only a metre or so away. "He was gorgeous and he fancies *you*." The other people at the table all looked about the same age, early twenties. There were five boys including Ravioli Man and three good-looking girls. I thought they all looked dead cool. Ravioli Man was modelling a Porn Star T and flared jeans – nice. The others were dressed in much the same garb. The girls wore trainers and jeans too. I suddenly felt over-dressed and glossed with my make-up and wedge sandals. We kept chatting amongst ourselves, looking over every now and then. One of the boys, with an eyebrow-piercing, smiled at me. He was really cute with David Beckham hair. "That one with the piercing's mine," Gemma whispered, staking her claim before anyone else had a chance.

"Shall we go back to the bar for some drinks?" she said in a really loud theatrical voice, after we'd paid the bill. Sam looked pained, her face catching up with her ears.

"Oh yes," said Katie. "Let's sit where we did before, by the bar." Jeeez, were these two auditioning for a part in a cheesy porn movie? If so, their Oscar cabinet would be as empty as their heads.

Sat back in the snug corner near the bar, we counted our money. "So how much have we spent so far?" Katie asked.

"Too much," I said. "We'd better slow down on the drink, 'cos we'll have to get a taxi home."

"If we order by the bottle, it works out cheaper." So that's what we did, and people became fuzzy and Gemma became louder. The music revved up a bit as the place filled up – I lost track of time. The tent was really buzzing when Ravioli Man and his friends arrived. There wasn't anywhere to sit except a table near us. So guess what happened next? I should have known there was going to be trouble. . .

chapter

ten

Something happens to time in Ibiza. One minute you're chatting away and it's only eleven at night and the next time you look at your watch, or watches if you are seeing double, it's nearly four in the morning and people are heading off for the next venue like they are just popping down the road to visit their granny. We were stuck in one of those time warps – I don't know where the evening went. The others sat down, we chatted, we had a few dances, we chatted some more and drank enough to sink a boat full of sumo wrestlers.

Sol (Ravioli Man) predictably made a beeline for our lovely Sam and introduced everyone. It turned out we had scored again on the meet and greet front, Sol and Matt (eyebrow-piercing) worked for Slinky Records, the most über-cool record store in Ibiza. Resuuullllt! I can't remember the names of all the others 'cos we were quite pissed by the time they sat down. It was someone's birthday and they were all out celebrating like us.

Katie, Gemma and I spent a lot of time chatting/slurring to Matt about the shop, clubs, where we could go out, getting the griff on the best places to experience Ibiza properly.

"Lilla DJs! Maybe she could come in on Monday and get some new tunes – you were saying that you were bored of the ones you had the other night, weren't you?" It was three in the morning and Katie was pissed – she had the thick tongue syndrome going on. She knew I hated talking about my DJing, especially as Dad went to the shop – Matt had already said he was a regular. Arse.

"Oh, d'you ever play out?" Matt asked.

"She should do, she's ace."

Thanks, Katie. "Oh, I'm still stuck in the

bedroom, though I did venture into the living room yesterday for a party. I don't play anywhere."

"Even so, come and see what we've got," he said kindly, sensing my reluctance to talk about it. "I'll pick you out a pile and you can take it from there."

Just then Gemma decided she'd had enough of sitting down and hauled Matt off to the dance floor – he glanced over his shoulder at me, mouthing, "Help!" He didn't stand a chance. Sam and Sol jumped up, too – they had been in a conference with a sign on the door all night: Do Not Disturb. It was just sooooo weird – I had never seen Sam actually talk to a boy the way she talks to us before, letting go and having a laugh.

"Come on, don't let me go on my own!" Matt shouted as he was dragged away.

"You're not, silly. You're with me," Gemma purred as she grabbed at his hand again, stumbling in her haste to hold it.

We all rocked down to the floor, which was heaving. Gemma was doing her best pole-dance routine. I noticed a few of the creepy olds from the table at dinner were trying to groove away (really trying, except it looked like Dad Dancing, you know – the parental two-step to *Club Tropicana*) and they kept bumping into Gemma.

She was so pissed she didn't notice. At first it looked like they didn't mean it, but after the third go, I knew they were being twats. I shouted "Hey!" but the music was so loud it just got swallowed up. No one else realized. Then Baldy executed a stunning sidestep, obviously thinking he was John Travolta or someone, and pushed his butt into Gemma while she was mid-gyration. Of course she went arse over tit and pulled me down with her.

I jumped up and pushed the old guy. "You knob. You did that deliberately!"

He turned and looked at me like I was mad. "Did what, *love*?" he shouted in a patronizing Londonesque gangsta drawl above the bass. "She's wasted, look at her!" And he pointed a mocking finger at Gemma who had fallen out of her boob tube, a pink puppy's nose poking out the top, hair stuck to her lip gloss. She looked like a car crash. I dragged her up off the floor.

"So what. That's no reason to push her over."

At this point Sam waded in with Sol. "Aahhh, it's the granddads. Getting revenge are we, 'cos we wouldn't accept your sleazy drink?" Sam was looking right at him. Sol was standing menacingly next to her, looking like a prizefighter.

"Do you need me to step in, Sam?" he growled menacingly. Katie and Matt suddenly noticed what was going on and helped swell our numbers.

Baldy went purple. "You'd better watch what you say, young lady. No one likes a smart arse." One of his cronies raised an arm and from nowhere came two brick shithouse security guards in tight black Ts and trousers, trampling people out of the way. Baldy spoke in Spanish to them. I understood enough to know he was stitching us up, saying we'd been hassling him and then got nasty 'cos we were so pissed. Typical teenage kids, etc, etc. Bastard.

"He says you causing trouble. Come with me." And Tweedledum started pushing Gemma and me off the dance floor.

Sam grabbed Tweedledee. "Those men were hassling our friends. They pushed her over," indicating Gemma, "all 'cos we wouldn't have a drink with them earlier."

Baldy jabbered in Spanish as Gem and I were frogmarched away. "He says your boyfriend was threatening him. I think you should come with us too." And Tweedledee tried to take Sol's arm, but he pulled it away and walked off the dance floor. Sam, Katie and Matt followed. It was like the

Gestapo. As soon as we got clear away from the dance floor, we were told we had to leave.

"But we haven't done anything wrong," I said; my head was starting to pound and I could feel the hangover fairy waving her evil wand. "We were hassled to death by those old men and they pushed Gemma over." Why did we sound like drunken brats? I wanted to scream: "It's not fair!" in a lispy voice.

"Can we get our stuff, PLEASE?" I asked in true sulky-teenager style. Get this – we were *escorted* to where we left our bags! The others were shocked and it was cripplingly embarrassing 'cos they were all older than us. My face was on fire – I just wanted to go home. Everyone came with us, it was nearly chucking out time anyway and the place had emptied a bit. As we walked out through the gallery I heard Sol ask Sam for her number.

"Look, we'll come in the shop and say hi, if you still want to see us," I said to Matt, itching to get my hands on some new records and testing the water to see if he thought we were a bunch of idiots. "I'm so sorry about tonight."

"No worries," he said. "This place can be a bit of a playboy's paradise at the weekends. Tossers."

We said goodbye and climbed in our cab.

Gemma stared out of the window at Matt. "He didn't ask for my number," she said forlornly. I didn't have the heart to say she was so pissed she'd probably scared him off. Sometimes, she really was a worry. I looked round and he was still staring at the cab. When he saw me look, he waved. I smiled to myself for some reason. He *was* cute, but obviously I didn't care, did I?

chapter

eleven

We were slumped on hired sunbeds near the beach bar Bora Bora – all in bikini bottoms, all feeling jaded from last night's activities. I was attempting to read a course book for Uni – it would have cured insomnia and it certainly wasn't helping my hangover. I mean, like who cares about some dysfunctional Scottish family that kills each other over a ruby brooch and then tries to blame it on the serfs uprising against the system? Don't get me started. Gemma thought I was mad: "I don't understand why you just can't do what you want. Why go to Uni when you know it's something you'll hate?" I couldn't explain. English was the thing I was least shit at. I felt like I *had* to do something. DJing was just a hobby, right? I couldn't do it for real, could I? Oooh – I DO NOT want to think about this now. . .

Meanwhile, in the real world . . . Platja D'en Bossa was the longest beach around and every available golden centimetre was taken up with a toasting body. The smell of suntan oil mingled with other substances hung like invisible fog in the heat. Behind us was a jumbled strip of bars and hastily put-up hotels that looked like prison cells, but Bora Bora was cool as, stretching right back from the beach with a rows of tables and drinks-label-emblazoned umbrellas in front of the bar. Their barmen were freelance research scientists, creating mind-altering cocktails that were beyond fabularse.

Everyone came here after the clubs closed so they could carry on, and on – the music was more chilled-out beats at this time of afternoon but still banging enough for people to be dancing on their sunbeds should they feel the need. And there were a few feeling the need, wearing spangly shorts, bikini glitter tops and angel wings and waving wands – leftover casualties from Space just over the road. You really felt like you were in some sort of docu-soap about the effects of excess on disenfranchised yoof (said in posh accent whilst wearing sandals *and* socks, yah?). It is such a seriously twenty-four/ seven place, you watch the wasted clubbers and preening queens for hours and actually feel quite normal sat there in your pink rubber catsuit, sweating.

Sam was engrossed in an *NME*, Katie in a Jackie Collins and Gemma was reading *Vogue*. Some guys were sunbathing nude, basting their little man in oil like a banger. Fried onions, anyone? Why did they *always* have pot bellies and hairy backs? I was dreading bumping into those creeps from last night, but we were well hidden here between a German couple who were rubbing oil on each other (get a room) and some Italian men who were gay. Who else would wear silver Speedos?

Bora Bora's like Aladdin's Cave, you could buy anything: food, drink, weed, speed, E, Charlie, Special K; you name it, there would be someone somewhere who knew a man who knew a dog who could sniff it out for you. I knew 'cos my dad has always warned me of the dangers of drugs, how easy they are to get hold of, especially here in Ibiza. But he has nothing to worry about – seeing the state he used to get in has put me off accidentally inhaling varnish fumes when I do my nails, let alone trying drugs. You'd have to be an idiot to go down that road.

"Uh-oh!" someone called out behind us. "Fancy bumping into you here!" The Speedo Kings turned round gawping and started rattling off in Italian. Andy stood above us, holding a towel and not much else, looking gorgeous, oblivious to the twitterings he'd caused next to us. "How are you, angels? Teasing the boys with your pert little butts?"

"Actually, I don't think any of the boys here fancy us," said Gemma, feigning sadness. "We did meet some nice boys last night, but I don't know when we'll see them again."

Andy slumped down on my bed near my feet. I turned over on to my back, feeling ridiculous worrying about him seeing my tits; he *was* gay. My fried eggs weren't going to make a tent in the trouser department. "So – how was the birthday?"

I'd told him we were going to Souk when he was at the villa and so I recalled the night's activities for him in detail.

"Oooh, ladies – you are devils." He stood up casting a shadow on my face. "Sounds like you need a drink to calm your nerves. What you having? They're on me – my friend Paulo runs the bar, he owes me a few freebies."

"Cocktails!" Gemma yelled. "Strong ones."

Day three in the movie of our holiday: oblivion beckons again. Cut to me looking yellow on a sunbed. "My liver's on crutches," I moaned. "Tomorrow we're having a day off – it's Sunday, for Christ's sake. Anyway, Sam and I have to ride the bikes back."

"But Ibiza never stops, darling. It's Sundays at Space tomorrow," he shouted over his shoulder as he headed to the bar.

"We're here for a month, we can do it next Sunday. We need to conserve money."

Ten minutes later and he brought over the umbrella-heavy *green* cocktails: "Zombies – they've got everything in them!" They tasted like Fruit Pastilles with the sharp kick of a drug-fuelled mule – delish.

"So, Katie, what's the griff on the evil ex?" asked

Andy settling on his towel in the sand – he was sooooooo muscly, nnnnnggggg.

"I got a text this morning asking if I was hungover. He sounded really pissed off."

"Oooh, boys!" he teased.

"He isn't used to you not doing what he wants, is he?" I said, risking a shoeing.

"He isn't used to me not being there when he wants me. Last night made me think a lot. I had such an ace time on my birthday, even though I missed him this morning when I felt flat. Then I got the text message and just thought, NO! You can't make me feel bad for having fun." Katie beamed, but I wasn't convinced she meant it – it could just be fighting talk. . .

"You know what this means, don'tcha?" asked Andy. "You need a whole new look to go with a whole new you!"

"Ooooooohhh, yes, yes, yes!" Gemma sat up, her magazine going flying. "Let me help! I think you should get your hair cut – it's too long for your face and your small body. And we should get you some really funky going-out clothes."

"What's wrong with my clothes?" Katie asked defensively.

"Nothing at all, but I think you should show off

your body more, not like Christina Aguilera, but subtly – look, there are some ideas in here." And she leaned over and picked *Vogue* up off the sand. Katie clambered over bodies and sat on Gem's bed where they discussed her new look.

"It's a classic," said Andy, offering round his fags and then sparking one up. He leaned back on his towel, his abs rippling under the suntan oil – oh, where do I look? "Girl dumps boy, suddenly she looks fab, has new hair, clothes – boy regrets everything he ever did." Looking thoughtful, he took a drag. "Katie, I know the man you should go and see for your hair – do you want me to call him now?"

A flick of an ear later and Katie was fixed up with Rio the Hair Architect, or whatever his title was, at Slice in Ibiza Old Town tomorrow. Gemma was going to be chief stylist and oversee the whole transformation. I think Katie secretly liked being fussed over.

"Here, Andy, can you rub some lotion on my back for us?" I asked, not quite believing my own cheek. Well, how else was I going to get those gorgeous hands all over me? They deffo put something in the air in Ibiza. . .

*

Sunday: Sam had a date, Katie had a makeover and I had a choice – go to Dad's or go with the girls and have an explore round the Old Town. Well, I was still not talking to him after his rant, even though he *had* called, not to apologize, you understand, but to see if I wanted to go round for Sunday lunch. It was like he'd never said I was crap at all! I blew him out for lunch; I wanted to mooch with the girls.

"How do I look?" Sam asked as she did up a beaded hippie necklace. I was cooking some sort of pasta thing for lunch – tomatoes, courgettes (no garlic on Sam's instructions!) and mushrooms. Everyone was hanging in the kitchen, all starving and waiting for food like circling vultures.

She was wearing a short denim Diesel mini with pockets at the front, red flip-flops and a red boob tube with a sequinned butterfly on the top right. She looked chilled and beautiful. Sol was going to wet himself.

"You look hubba hubba, but not desperado," I said.

"Cool – and can you see the zit on my chin?"

"What zit? There isn't one. Surely 'mates' don't care about zits, anyway."

"Yeah, well. Zits are zits – minging." And she

was back to her usual glacial self. Sol had rung last night when we'd got home after our day at the beach. He'd said he was taking her to a mate's bar in town after he finished work and we were all going down to hang out with her beforehand while Katie had her hair cut. Just as "friends", Sam was careful to point out. Friends, my arse – no garlic anyone?

chapter

twelve

Sam and I'd got bored in Slice, the painfully trendy hairdressers – lime-washed wood floors, chrome here, there and everywhere and a DJ spinning tunes at the back! There're only so many *OK Magazines* you can read without bumping into my dad. So we went for a wander while Katie was getting the chop. Gemma was advising at the same time as flirting like a hooker on speed with everyone in there, whether they were straight or not (not, mostly).

We wandered round the shops, checking out the clothes (cheap) and bars (millions of them), picking up flyers for club nights for the next week. After a lightning tour of Dalt Villa – the walled area at the top (beautiful ancient windy streets, little bars and restaurants, picture galleries, lots of steps, blisters) – we returned to Slice to pick up Katie from Rio's clutches.

"Oh, you look shit hot!" Sam exclaimed when we walked in. Her hair was cut into a bob ending just under her chin with a sloping fringe. She'd had honey highlights, streaks like natural sunkissed gold. It lit up her whole face.

"Yes, I've washed that boy right outta my hair!"

"Sheeeez so beautiful, all the hair, it was hiding her face. Now you can see her!" Rio was as camp as a row of pink chiffon tents, fussing all over her like she was a china doll. His blond spiky hair looked like a transplant on top of his black face. "Maybe we can do you next, eeh?" And he lifted up a tuft of sweaty hair from my head. Cheek!

"No, we have to go now," I said. I didn't want anything done to my hair – it was short enough already and I could see a mad glint in his eye. He would probably turn me into a ginger if I didn't escape. Katie kissed him goodbye and Gemma kissed everyone, even customers.

"I think maybe the DJ was straight," she said laughing. "He kept winking at me."

"Yes, but he was a minger," Katie said.

It was nearly time for Sam to meet Sol so we left her to walk there, and Gemma still hadn't finished with Katie.

"Gem, do you mind riding one of the bikes back? I'm going to go now 'cos I've looked in all the shops and can't afford anything. I'm going to catch the last rays at home."

I'd been reading by the pool for an hour when Andy turned up to see how the makeover had gone. Katie had rung him to let him know they'd be back in a bit and he popped in on his way out to meet some friends for dinner. We were just getting into a juicy convo about how he'd told his mum he was gay when music suddenly blasted out of the living room, and Gemma walked down the steps dressed like a porn star, but a classy one, you understand. They'd returned from the shops.

"Ladies and gentlemen and Lilla, I introduce to you the new-look Katie."

She waved her arms dramatically as Katie arrived behind her at the top of the steps and slunk down them to the opposite side of the pool to parade up and down the imaginary catwalk. She looked like Kylie! Andy and I screamed like idiots.

Katie grinned. She was wearing the pink shorts I'd bought her and a new top made of black spangly mesh with a built-in bra. It floated out behind her. Hiding in her hair was a pair of gigantic silver hoop earrings. She was a pop star, no doubt about it. Her cork wedge heels were almost falling off as she did a sexy little dance to the music, shimmied back the way she'd come and then took a bow, winking suggestively.

Andy and I ran over to her. "Those dancers in Pacha better watch out 'cos you were hot, lady!" He gave her a big kiss.

"Katie! You cow – you look like a princess! You should have cut your hair years ago. And wow – your make-up." I was bowled over.

She was glowing. "Yes, Gemma did it. I love it." It was all sparkly on the eyes with big lashes and glossy lips and shimmery cheeks. "You should see what else I bought – some really cool stuff from the boutiques. Everything is so much cheaper here than at home. My birthday money went much further than in London."

"Can you do me?" I asked Gemma. "I want to look like that when we next go out."

"Any time, my services are free to friends and good-looking boys. All we need now is to fix this sexy girl up with someone."

"Oh, Gemma, no! I'm not sure. . ." Katie whimpered. Tom's nasty whiff was obviously still lingering.

"Katie — we're not talking marriage, just a snog." Gemma rolled her eyes, not understanding at all.

Monday — another perfect Ibizan morning, air so clear you could see every leaf on every tree. Katie and I flopped by the pool until lunchtime, reading crap mags and toasting. We'd had a civilized evening the previous night with a few bottles of wine and a yummy barbecue prepared by Katie. Gemma still hadn't got up and we didn't expect to see Sam until the evening at least. She'd come in really late last night and had crashed around a bit, sounding like her coordination was taking a bit of a bashing. Always a sign of a good night!

My moby went at about one — I didn't recognize

the number at all. "Err, is that Lilla?" a male voice asked nervously.

"Yeah, who's this?"

"Matt from Slinky." Ohhhh – what did he want? "I got your number off Sam."

"Oh?"

"She came in the shop last night and said I should call you – we've just had some wicked tunes in. D'you want to come down and listen to them? I've put a load by."

"Yeah, cool, that would be excellent. What time?"

"Now?" I necked the Coke Katie had just handed me and told her we were off on a road trip. We left the others a note. New tunes always excited me!

"Here she is!" Sol called when I walked in half an hour later with Katie. He stood at the back behind the counter – Matt was serving someone. "We've got a pile for you, young lady, under the counter." The shop was cool as. Racks and racks of tunes, all with pointer cards and genre and sub-genre sections: House, Disco, Funky House, Hardcore, Trance, This Week's Recommended, Biggest Tune, US Garage, US

House, Chicago House, Electro, UK Garage. Along the right-hand side were five turntables with headphones so you could listen before you bought. My skin started tingling. People turned when I came up to the counter – it was quite busy, filled mostly with men and boys, a few touristy people too. Maybe they thought I was someone.

"Hi! This's really kind of you."

"No problem. How's Sam?" Sol grimaced, holding his head.

"Yeah, we haven't seen her since she went out last night. I guess she's really hungover, too."

"At least she doesn't have to be at work," he moaned.

"Sol – if you can't stand the heat, don't play with fire, or something like that," Matt laughed, coming up behind him. "Hi, Lilla, Katie. Check these out." And he slammed down a pile of about fifty records. "Happy listening, if you want more, just shout." He walked back to the till where someone was waiting to pay.

"Did Sam tell you about the bar on Tuesday?" Sol asked. I shook my head. "We're all going out to this new place that has good DJs. You can dance – it's like a club except you don't pay the extortionate amount to get in. It's run by the same people that do Space on Sunday." I wasn't going to turn down a night like that and I knew the others wouldn't either.

"Katie, you don't have to stay," I said while we waited for a free deck.

"What else am I going to do? Can't I help and listen too? One ear each on the phones?" So we ploughed our way through. Matt brought us over some Cokes, what a sweetie. "He likes you," Katie whispered.

"Don't be ridiculous. He's just being friendly."

"No one else gets Cokes with a smile." She giggled, and I looked up and he was staring right at me. He looked away quickly and started unpacking a box. Naaah, he was probably just checking out Katie's new hair.

An hour later we had whittled the pile down to about fifteen records but there was no way I could afford all of them. I picked the best ten and left it at that.

"Is that all you're getting?" Matt asked when I went up to pay.

"It's all I can afford."

He flicked through them. "You chose some right banging ones. Here, why don't you get those other five you really want, they're excellent, and I'll give you those ones half price?"

"Are you sure?" He was REALLY nice.

"Don't look a gift horse in the mouth. Of course. You've got to have those tunes as well. It wouldn't be right." And he winked. He actually winked at me. I could feel myself go red. Oh no, ground, eat me now.

"I told you," Katie whispered as he stuffed them in two bags.

"Thank you. We'll see you tomorrow I expect, when Sam feels better."

"Yeah, deffo. Break a leg."

I looked at him, what did he mean? Break a leg? "Lilla, I was wondering if –" he started to say, but I switched off 'cos it was drowned out by a familiar geezer laugh: Dad.

"All right, Stevo," I heard Sol say and they did this high five across the counter to the right of me. Dad had his shades on like a typical DJ and was oblivious to me 'cos I obviously wasn't anyone important.

"Quick, Katie, we have to leave now," and I ran out the shop, leaving Matt open-mouthed, in my haste catching my vest on one of the record racks. There was this ripping sound and I felt my top flatten my tits and then ping as it ripped properly and came loose. I rocketed forward like I'd been shot from a cannon and just carried on hurtling out the door.

"Lilla! You forgot your bag," Matt called after my retreating back. Arse. How could I go back? My left boob was hanging out and Dad would see it was me. Why was my life like an episode of *Jackass TV*?

"Are you mad – Matt will think you're a right weirdo now!" Katie complained, catching up with me as I waited round the corner, trying unsuccessfully to tie my top together.

"Didn't you see? It was Dad – he was standing right next to us."

"Then it's lucky I rescued these then, wasn't it?" she said, holding up the bag.

"Thank you! I'm sorry. I couldn't handle another row." It was sod's law Dad came in at the same time. "What d'you think Matt meant by 'break a leg'?" I asked remembering.

"I have no idea. Look – what do you think of these trousers in Zara?" And she dragged me inside before I could ask any more questions. And what was the other thing he was going to ask me? I'd never know, 'cos how could I even look at him tomorrow? Oh, the shame. . .

chapter
thirteen

When we got back, Gem and Sam were up, lying in the shade under umbrellas with sunglasses on and pints of water handy.

"I feel so hungover," Sam replied, when I asked her how her date went, evading the question. "What happened to your top?"

"Oh, nothing, I caught it on a nail." I couldn't be arsed to even tell them.

"Did you see the gorgeous Matt? Did he ask about me?" Gemma asked mischievously.

"No, but he was quite busy." Maybe that's what he was going to ask about – Gemma. That made sense.

"Shall we make something to eat?" Katie asked.

"Yes, please," Gem and Sam both chimed and Gemma jumped up to crack open a bottle of red – any excuse!

Katie and I set to work making Spag Bol – the total hangover cure-all. Over dinner Sam told us about her evening. "I was really nervous about meeting Sol 'cos I really like him." We all went, "Aaaah." "I know, I know, unusual for me. Well, he took me to a few trendy small bars at the back of the town where some of the DJs were really good and we were getting into the music and I realized that I was liking him more and more and it made me feel tongue-tied and stupid. This is why I NEVER go out with boys, 'cos they always make me feel like that if I like them. I was convinced he would think I was dead boring, so I downed some tequila shots on top of the red wine I'd already drunk to loosen me up. We went on somewhere else and ordered another bottle of wine and then another, and suddenly I was feeling really floaty and giggly and having a real laugh. We danced and I really wanted him to kiss me and then I can't remember any more. Apart from a taxi driver telling me I was home and being sick outside the gate. When I woke up this morning something had died in my mouth. What a loser." She shook her head. "Sol must think I'm such a tosser."

"No, he doesn't. He didn't say anything when we saw him in the shop. He was feeling hungover too, and I'm sure he still likes you," Katie reassured her. "Anyway, you're going to see him tomorrow night."

"Like he'll turn up! I don't think so." She looked really pissed-off with herself. "I feel like I'm in a bed of nails sandwich with an elephant sitting on top. I never knew self-loathing could reach such dizzy heights."

"But did you snog him?" Gemma asked.

"That's it, I don't know! How can I face him if I don't know that?"

"You'll be able to tell. He'll look different, won't he?" Gemma said wisely.

"Or he might pretend it never happened," Sam lamented. So both Sam and I would be wearing the Shirt of Shame tomorrow. At least I wasn't on my own.

I got on the decks and played my new tunes —

they were wicked. Real stonkers and they went well with a few of my faves from home. The others boogied while they loaded the dishwasher. "You know, Lilla, you really should try and get a gig. There are lots of these open-deck nights on at the moment," Sam said again.

"I know, I know. I will when I feel ready." But when would that be?

Music blasted out of the speakers waking me with a start. Facing me on the dressing table was a red-nosed gnome holding up a piece of paper that said GET UP! "OK, OK!" I moaned at it. Since when did gnomes do wake-up calls? Katie was in the pool doing laps; Gemma was making a huge breakfast of fried bacon, eggs, mushies and toast. Sam was laying the table outside and two gnomes were balancing a basket of fresh pastries and glazed bread rolls on their heads – yum. I could smell the fresh coffee wafting through the hatch and into the garden. "Wow, everyone's so busy. What do you want me to do?"

"Nothing – it's all done. Just sit down and relax. You've – we've got a big night tonight and we've got to conserve our energy. Katie – brekkie's nearly ready!"

"What do we want to do today?" asked Sam after we'd cleared away the dishes.

"Why don't we go to Salines beach?" Gemma suggested. "It's supposed to be the poshest one around – all the beautiful people go there." We all agreed on it. "Don't forget we have to get back here, though, to get ready – I promised Lilla I'd do a makeover for tonight."

"Oh, don't worry about me. I'll just wash and go."

"NO!" all three of them cried.

"I mean, Katie will be all done up, so will Sam and I, so you must too!"

"Why, what's this place we're going to? A celeb hang-out or something?"

"Yes," Gemma shot back. "So it's glitter all round."

Salines beach – home of the perfect eight. Hello hang-ups! Embrace them – love your wobbly thighs! BUT body-swerve the place if you worry about cellulite craters in your bum or bingo wing arms. Everywhere we looked there was some mahogany babe in spangly bikini bottoms the size of a Band Aid prancing and flicking her hair, with super-skinny super-smooth limbs, not a dimple on show and the most pert pair of tits you ever saw. WoMAN was NOT created equal... It was boy heaven. No wonder they were all lying on their stomachs...

We had parked the mopeds near the Jockey Club beach bar where the DJ was spinning chunky tunes. Hence all the prancing by the beach Amazonians. All the sunbathers looked foreign, not a pale bod or freckle in sight – or an England shirt! "Are we sure we want to stay here?" Katie asked, pulling a face. "Just look at everyone, and people down the far end look naked."

"Fuckem!" Gemma barked. "We look great and they're all going to get skin cancer anyway 'cos they're so brown!" And she swung her bag on to her shoulder and sashayed down the gentle slope away from the pine trees and bar and on to the narrow strip of pure white sand. The sea was postcard-blue, with quite a few rocks that you'd have to pick your way over before you could swim properly. There were windsurfers pulled up on the sand and out in the ocean, yachts of all shapes and wealthiness bobbed up and down in the gentle breeze. Millionaires' row. "Come on!"

Gemma found a spot not far from the bar in between two groups of boys – typical. "We need to be where we can get beers." A few heads turned when she marched down the beach. She fitted right in with the beautiful people in her Holy Grail of bikinis – the gold Princess Leia one – and hair scraped back into two plaits under a fake Burberry headscarf. I looked down at the faded pink sarong covering my hips and sucked in my tummy; the others did the same.

We sizzled, we dipped in the Zombie-green sea, we sizzled some more, we batted off unsuitable boys who couldn't speak any English and wore enough jewellery to put P Diddy to shame, and all the effort made our tummies rumble. "Let's hit the Jockey Club," Sam said, getting up and tying her sarong in a complicated manner about her person. "I need a beer and something yummy."

It was time to people-watch as we sat elevated, overlooking the bodies, shaded from the rays by a canvas canopy, a delicious breeze drying our dripping hair. I ordered a pitcher of Pimms to get us in the holiday mood and we asked for Greek Salads all round. Yum. I was aware of a table of older people behind us, but they weren't so close we felt crowded. Just as the waiter brought the drinks over and took our food orders, I heard a glass clinking like someone was going to make a speech. I looked up as one of them cleared his throat and felt sick to my silver toenails. It was the baldy guy from Souk. The others had noticed too. He was wearing another extremely expensive ghetto-fabulous shirt – he looked so wrong. And his forehead was even redder and shinier than before. "Oh, shit," Gemma whispered, and slid under the table as far as she could.

"My thoughts exactly. Maybe if we just keep quiet and don't get up to go to the loo, he won't notice us. There are so many people here."

I didn't see if any of the other olds were there, 'cos I didn't want to catch Baldy's eye. We carried on giving everyone grades out of ten on the sand and sipping Pimms with our eyes firmly on the beach and away from the table.

"This isn't fair – he was the one who was in the wrong," Sam fumed, "and here we are hiding like it's our fault."

"Just leave it," Katie said. "What's the point of stirring something up just for the sake of it?"

Our food arrived mid-speech and we all kept eyes down and faces turned away. He was winding it up though I couldn't hear what he was saying, but I heard the toast: "To Lena and Steve!" And the table responded back, raising their glasses.

Fuckity fuck. Out of the frying pan and into the deep-fat fryer with the lid pressed down.

"Eeeek," was all Katie could say.

Dad stood up, but luckily he had his back to us – he hadn't seen us come in. Lena was sitting next to him, looking up, all adoring. My mistake was looking round to see if he was going to spot us and catching Baldy's eye. Arse. He squinted, and then he recognized me and sneered. Dad said thank you to everyone and said they'd let them know about the wedding plans, all invites were in the post, etc, etc, blah, blah. Wedding plans? WEDDING????? What wedding?

"We've been spotted." And just as I said it, old Baldy got up and came over, drink in hand.

"We really should stop meeting like this, ladies. I would offer you a drink, but I'd be afraid of getting beaten up." And he laughed, standing there like a dwarf in a high-jump competition.

"Why don't you just fuck off," Sam said under her breath.

"What did you say?" he spat.

"You heard." And she glared right back at him, defiant.

"Are you causing trouble over there, Dave?" Dad joked. "Annoying the young girls again, you old – Philippa!" He was standing behind Dave, hand on his shoulder in a matey catalogue stance.

"You *know* these little bitches?" Dave slurred. Yep, drunk again.

Dad didn't say anything. Shit was going to hit the fan any second now. I could see the mental Steve Wheeler vein throbbing at his left temple. "Bitches?" he said in the menacing tone that sent me running for the nuclear bunker the few times I'd heard it.

"Yeah, bitches. This one," he pointed at me, "pushed me over the other night when I was just minding my own business. She was drunk and out of control. Mouthy too, all of them."

"Call my daughter a bitch one more time and I'll give you a push you won't get up from. Sit down!" And Dad took his hand off Dave's back and looked right at me. "Philippa, what's been going on?"

Dave was catatonic with embarrassment and horror and sat back down straight away. The other table was now engrossed in the unfolding family drama. "How did I guess you would assume this was all my fault?" I fumed.

"I didn't say it was, but pushing over men in clubs when you're falling-down drunk? Didn't anything I say ever sink in?"

"She wasn't drunk, Mr Wheeler," Katie stuck up for me, bless her.

"Did I ask you, Katie?" Instant sunburn for Katie. "Philippa? Are you going to tell me why one of my friends thinks you're a bitch?"

"Why? You won't believe me anyway." I looked at Sam and she knew immediately and started gathering our bags. "Ask Baldy over there why he tries it on with kids young enough to be his daughter and then see why he 'fell over'!" I stood up and so did the others. Deep breaths. *Please don't cry*, I begged myself. . . "Oh, and thanks for the wedding invite, Dad!"

"Philippa, come back here!" Dad shouted at my retreating back. "I want this cleared up, NOW!"

"Run to the mopeds," I said under my breath and we legged it without paying the bill, the waiter only just realizing as we reached the bottom of the steps. Great, now he was after us. I jumped on one bike and Sam on the other, helmets rammed on heads. I don't know who was on the back of mine, but I couldn't get the key in the ignition, my hands were shaking so much. "Come on, come on," I chanted, finally slotting it in, turning it and revving like I was in motocross. We took off to a flying start, nearly running over two boys who walked in front at the wrong time. "Sorrrrry!" Gemma shouted from behind me. I could hear the waiter yelling – he was chasing us. "Faster!" Gemma was screaming. "He's going to get us!" Sam was neck and neck with me – it was hard to go really fast on the rubble road, but I managed it and so did Sam, leaving the mad waiter behind in a cloud of dust and pebbles. We did it and in minutes we were creaming along the main road back to Ibiza Town. "Lilla – you maniac!" Gemma shouted above the buzzing hairdryer. She said something else but I couldn't hear, I was too busy trying to blink away the tears blurring my vision and sniff back up my nose the snot that was threatening to cascade down to my chin. What a mess. . .

chapter

fourteen

"Please Lilla, we promised everyone we'd go out tonight. It won't be the same without you." Katie sat at the end of the bed while I lay on it, a cloud of self-pity hovering over me.

"Katie, I've just had the shittest day so far and going out isn't going to help." It was still the afternoon and the others were in the pool, I could hear them laughing, reliving the Great Escape. We'd been back about an hour. "I just need to chill and not have to go anywhere where those tossers might be."

"I promise, they won't be at this place – it's far too trendy and cool and probably wouldn't let them in. Please! Matt's going."

Maybe yesterday that would have been a carrot, but after my tit-baring in Slinky and the shock news and runner today it wasn't really that appealing. Dad was being his usual self, thinking he knew everything about everyone and jumping to conclusions. I should have known Dave would be one of his friends. He was probably going to be Dad's best man. The more I thought about it, the more I wanted to smack him in the face. Dad, that is, for not thinking of me again. That was the straw and I was the camel in a back-brace.

There was a buzzing at the gate – someone was outside. "I'll go," Katie said.

I heard footsteps coming down the corridor. I couldn't face Dad. Another argument would finish me off. But it was Lena.

"Hi, Philippa. Are you OK?"

"What do you care?" I grumbled looking at the wall. Aha, Dad sent the understudy to do his dirty work.

"I know you must be very angry. I am so, so sorry you had to hear about the wedding like that. Your dad has no idea I'm here. He's at home gathering the courage to come over here. He feels terrible. Even if you did leave him with the bill." She laughed nervously and sat on the edge of the bed, inspecting her immaculate French manicure.

"He hasn't exactly read the *Good Father Handbook*, has he? When were you going to tell me about the wedding?" I could feel my voice wobble. I wasn't going to cry in front of her. No way.

"The plan was to tell you at Sunday lunch – but you cancelled. So whenever you were around. I wanted your dad to tell you this morning, but Dave forced us into this lunch. He's his best man, you see."

"That's just great! Not only is his best man a total bastard, Dad believes I decked him in a club!"

"Dave's a troublemaker, he's got your father into tight spots so many times it's beyond a world record." Tell me something that would shock me. "He's a dabbler, fingers in lots of pies in clubland, but he's helped your dad out of some financial difficulties this year. If it wasn't for that, I would have kiboshed him a long time ago."

"But Dad doesn't need him now, does he?"

"No, but your dad couldn't see that. He thinks he's fun, harmless, but I think he's had a wake-up call today. The position of best man might just have become vacant." She stood up. "I'm going to go, don't tell your dad I came." I nodded. "I wanted you to know he didn't want you to be upset about him getting married." And she tried to give me something, but I wouldn't take it. She sighed and left the room.

Katie came in when she'd gone. "Are you all right?"

"Yeah."

Katie picked up something from the bedside cabinet. "Lilla! She's given you a hundred quid in Euros!"

I sat up smiling, the clouds dispersed and it was sunny once again. "Well, I guess the drinks are on me, then!" I could think about this another time. Yeah, yeah, I'm easily bought. . .

If someone had told me what I would be doing this evening a few hours ago, I would have refused to come out. I hadn't suspected a thing, not even when Gemma insisted I wear her best outfit – sequinned pink boob tube and tight white hipsters with sequins on the pocket. She did my make-up and hair, and I have to admit that I looked amazing for me. I just thought they were being nice after what had happened earlier.

Dad made an appearance just as we were about to get into a taxi – convenient, huh? He grovelled in a slightly huffy "It's not my fault" manner that he has about everything he fucks up. Almost making the grovelling worthless. Anyway, I agreed to have lunch with them tomorrow.

We met everyone for drinks in the Base Bar on the marina – it was busy even that early. Families mixed with clubbers and older barflies in the strip that faced the boats on the water. The sun went down, making the flashing signs, fairy lights and candles seem all the more alluring. Each bar had tables outside and they all blended into one giant bar, or it seemed like it. Matt and Sol were already there when we arrived.

I felt my cheeks burn when I saw Matt, but he acted cool, maybe even a little cold. He did think I was a twat! Sam was quiet, but Sol stepped up from his seat so she could sit down, so I guess at least she didn't have anything to worry about. Gemma was more hyper than usual, if that's possible, and Katie was ultra quiet. "Are you all right?" I asked. "You seem all nervous. It's not Tom again, is it? Has he been calling you?"

"No, thank God. I'm fine, honestly." She didn't look it, sipping her drink and not really joining in.

She kept looking at her watch too. Matt sat the other side of the tall table; he looked fit tonight in his twisted jeans and T with a pic of Seventies icons CHiPs on the front.

I started singing the theme tune and he laughed. "I thought no one ever watched that."

"I love all that cheese. You can get it on Sky. I used to be in love with Ponch when I was about six," and we ended up having a stupid conversation about who we fancied when we were little. At least he was talking to me now. Hopefully I could forget about yesterday completely. Sol and Sam were getting on really well again and I noticed she only had one Zombie this time!

I spotted Gemma ogling Matt. Obviously Operation Get a Snog was being planned and final details being checklisted. She butted in right when we were laughing about crushes on kids' TV presenters and newsreaders (strange boy).

"So, Matt, when was the last time you had a proper snog then, not just fantasy ones?" Jeeez — she had no shame.

"I can't remember," he laughed, embarrassed. "Too long ago." Obviously he was hoping to score with Gemma tonight, the way he'd gone bright red.

"Oh, I don't believe that for a second," she flirted, steering the convo towards her.

Hello — excuse me! I *am* here, Gemma. I *was* talking to him before you rudely hijacked the situation, I fumed silently. Why was I getting my knickers in a twist? She was so obviously after him, what else did I expect? The Man-Eater was in full flow, stand back amateurs, the pro was gonna show us how it was done. . .

At about ten Sam started rounding us up, and we headed off to the next place, the U Bar, which was set further back from the bustling marina. As we were standing up, I could hear a commotion at the far end of the marina to our right. "Oh, cool — it's the Privilege parade!" Gemma gasped. We didn't have a choice but to watch as it marched past, tourists diving out of the way. Statuesque drag queens carried placards telling us all what night it was at the club, how many free drinks you could get, DJs playing, that sort of thing. Half-naked muscle men were painted a silvery blue with the Privilege logo painted in black on their chests. I noticed a few dwarfs carrying torches, nearly setting fire to one man's bum at the Base Bar. A man dressed as a devil handed me a flyer.

"Look, next Monday it's Manumission. We

should go for my birthday," I said as we crossed the path carved by the parade. Gemma picked up a flyer off the pavement.

"Can we? It's got a live sex show!" Obviously hoping to get some tips. . .

"Ladies," Sol addressed us, "Manumission is full of real grotbags and tourists. You'd be better off going to Pacha."

We were ambling through the crowds, Sam leading the way with Katie. "But we *have* to experience it once, we don't have to stay all night."

"Let me see if I can get you on a guest list then, 'cos there's no point paying fifty quid and then leaving after a few hours. Leave it with me." What an absolute star. I grabbed him and gave him a smacker on the cheek. "No promises," he laughed.

U Bar looked like an ordinary hang-out from the outside, with big windows and a bouncer on the door. We went in and it was rammed to the rafters. The bar itself was like an old chemist counter: dark, curved wood stretching the length of the space, with a million and one bottles glistening behind it. It was two people deep already. Opposite that was an empty fireplace with a grand country-manor mantelpiece carved from marble, and above that the most colossal gilt mirror I had ever seen. It went right up to the celestial ceiling, upon which were painted fluffy clouds and pale blue sky. The floor was covered in mini red-and-white mosaic tiles — it was totally unlike anywhere else we had been so far in Ibiza.

"Pretty cool, huh?" Sam asked. The space was peppered with chunky wooden tables and bistro-style chairs, and the odd leather sofa here and there, and right at the back was the reason we were here, the DJ booth. It was on a raised platform and a small dance floor lay below it. It was built to look a bit like a Wurlitzer jukebox. Gemma found some tables near the dance floor while I went to the bar with Katie. Time to spend Lena's money.

Just as we were sitting down, one of the barmen leaped behind the decks and spoke to the DJ playing, and then went over to a guy sitting with a few mates near to the platform. "It's an open-deck night," Sam shouted above the bass. "All the DJs have already been booked for half an hour each. Thought you might want to see what the competition was like."

I did! The next guy was OK. His mixing needed a bit of work, and a few times it didn't hang together, but he was up there, having a go and he seemed to be loving it which was the main thing. I listened for a bit. No one was really dancing, they were all just chatting and drinking, feet tapping. After a while someone shouted my name. The barman was squatting down next to me. "Hey, Lilla, you're next after Duncan has finished." He waited for me to say something. He'd be waiting a long time. . . Tumbleweed brain. Did he just say what I thought he said?

"What do you mean?" How did he even know my name?

"Well, we have a slot for you to have a go on the open deck. It's all yours."

"I don't have any records with me."

"You do, they're behind the decks," Sol broke in. "I brought them down this afternoon."

The fog lifted. I looked round from the guy and they were all staring at me, anxious looks on their faces. Katie had gone white and Sam grimaced. No wonder Katie had been all silent, she was shitting herself for me. "You're on in about five minutes. If you want." I didn't know what to say. The bottom fell out of my stomach and all the Zombies I'd drunk felt like they were going to projectile all over the table.

"She'd love to." Sam stood up and came over.

The others all looked on. "Come on, Lilla, your records are there. Sol brought your headphones too. It'll be just like at the villa. No big deal." The barman nodded and went to tell Duncan I would be on after him.

"No big deal! NO BIG DEAL! Are you mad? I can't do this. I haven't prepared." I looked up at her but she wasn't listening.

"Lilla, my give-a-shitometer's on zero. I suggest you get up there and show us what you can do. You're brilliant and you know you are, so just do it." I wanted to cry, punch her in the face, anything but get up there and do it. The thing is, I knew she was right. I'd been running away from this for ages.

"Lilla, I've heard you're amazing. You'd be silly not to give it a shot. We've been looking forward to this all day in the shop." Matt looked right at me and I knew he meant it. And not in a "We can't wait to see you make a tit of yourself" way.

"Yes, let's show the boys what us girls are made of," Gemma shouted across the table.

So I stood up and wobbled over on my jelly legs. Duncan was just bringing in another tune, one I knew, and thought I had. He saw me and smiled. "That deck is on that channel and the other on the other. Press that for the headphones and *that* is the gains control for each channel, pretty simple really. Have fun!" And he unplugged his phones and asked me to put the record in its sleeve when I took it off and pointed to his record bag. I just looked at him in a glazed way, not taking in anything he said. Arghhhhhhhhhh! Now it was just me and my records and I had to make people dance. . .

chapter

fifteen

The mixer, I can't work the mixer — it was even more complicated than Jules's! If I survive this baptism of fire, I am personally going to torture all three of those witches on the dance floor. This was going to be the biggest balls-up of the new millennium. "Go Lilla! Go Lilla!" Gemma started chanting, but I froze her with an icy glare from behind the decks. Concentrate, Wheeler. You can do this.

I bent down, pulling up tune after tune, all the

new ones were in there, I chose one I thought would go and listened in the phones – I couldn't hear it, shit, where was it? The panic fairy started fluttering in my chest. I was convinced the other turntable was going to run out of beats any second now as the needle skidded to the centre of the record. I looked frantically across all the flashing lights and spotted the button to press. Phew, I could hear the tune – but it wasn't right! Think, think, you know what will go, so put it on! A record jumped into my hands and I ripped it from its sleeve and jammed it over the spindle on the empty deck. It sounded good, a few adjustments with the EQs. . . I slowed the pitch down slightly so the heartbeats were in synch. I was in the mix. The other record was stripping down to the bare bones – not good, not good at all, it would be a rushed mix before the horse left the stable. Everyone knows that's bad. I slid the fader across and the new tune came in, but it was way too loud – I'd forgotten to check the sound levels and it drowned out the previous one, but at least it hadn't sounded like a stampede.

The girls were cheering, I looked up and pulled a face, Sam nodded at me and pulled the same face back – it *had* sounded shit. But I knew now I could do it. It was only the mixer freaking me out. I chose another tune, a real funked-up crowd-pleaser and put it on, bringing it in, teasing the crowd (well, Gemma, Katie, Sam and a few other girls, the boys were at the bar). The mix was good, I was doing it, I was being a DJ somewhere other than Katie's bedroom! Now I relaxed and started to think more than one record ahead and pulled up a few. I only had half an hour, but I felt like I could play for ever. More people were getting up and dancing, the boys had got up. Everyone was really getting down and the dance floor almost filled up. All right!

Five minutes later it was all over! I got the signal and put on my last tune; some geeky guy from Edinburgh was on after me. He was gangly with thick, black-rimmed specs and floppy brown hair. And he had a massive zit on his chin. "Cool. Cool, maaaan," he mumbled as I showed him everything. "Like, you could mix and everything. . ." He sounded surprised, cheeky fucker.

I looked at the card in my hand as we left the bar. "Lilla, watch out!" Katie guided me around the tables. Outside the air smacked me in the face and the whole night threatened to overwhelm me.

"I think I'm pissed," I slurred to anyone who would listen.

"Yep, you are," Matt said coming up behind me and Katie with an arseholed Gemma tagged on to his arm as we wandered towards a taxi rank. She'd been homing in on him like a heat-seeking missile all night and I think he'd cracked 'cos they'd been dancing non-stop. She was grinning; it finally looked like Matt might have bitten the carrot. She wasn't used to boys playing it so cool. I knew Katie was wrong about him, he'd fancied Gemma all along, I could tell. Did I care? Not really, I had bigger fish to fry, no time to worry about boys. . . Sam was hand in hand with Sol right at the back. I was sure they had disappeared at one point in the evening for a game of tonsil hockey.

The trouble was, everyone had bought me drinks after my triumph on the decks so I wasn't sure what anyone had got up to, apart from dancing like loons and knocking back shots – or maybe that was just me? After the bottle of champagne, Matt had ordered cocktails and then the weirdest thing happened. I was already on my way to the hangover hall of fame when a guy came up to the group and started talking to me.

"I thought you were great," he smiled. I looked

at him, sniffing out sleazy chat-up lines. "No, seriously –" he could tell I was wearing my bullshit detector – "your DJing was class."

"Thanks," I said primly. He had the potential to be another Dave 'cos he was thirty-something, but good-looking blond without the shiny red forehead and receding hair. He reached into his jeans – he was wearing very trendy surfy clothes, not like Puff Daddy-loving Dave – and pulled out a card and handed it to me.

"I'm Charlie and I run Bar Lorca on the strip by the marina." Where was this going? "I think you'd be great for my punters – they'd love you and your music, just what I'm looking for."

"What? You want me to play in your bar?" Holy cow, Batman!

"Yes. Listen, have a think about it, it would be weekdays, Tuesdays and maybe Thursday evenings, three hours each time. My number's on there, give us a call tomorrow when you've recovered from your hangover," and he chuckled.

"Wow. Thank you. I will." He winked at me, then and shot off through the crowd and disappeared. Had that really happened? Did someone actually think I could be a DJ? I couldn't take it in. I showed Katie the card, just so it would feel real.

"That's amazing! I'm sooo pleased. You can get a job! Stay all summer!"

"Hang on, I haven't even got there yet."

Sol overheard. "That's great! Bar Lorca's not a bad bar, quite a few people cut their teeth there before going on to bigger and better things. You'll be fine."

The rest of the night passed in a blur of awful mixing until the resident came on. Girls dressed as immaculate short-skirted air hostesses paraded round the bar handing out free lollipops for those suffering the too-many-drugs desert-mouth syndrome, and tequila shots at a price for those of us wanting to dance with the devil. Sol made me have three – honest, he put a gun to my head. Tequila tastes the same coming up as going down.

Gemma and Matt were surgically attached and Katie was gyrating with some blond Tom looky-likey who was buying her drinks. Meanwhile, I was getting chatted up left right and centre. Apparently being a DJ ups your stakes on the sexometer. Unfortunately, none of the boys were remotely a five or six on the scale – the lowest grade I was allowing myself to go. Best chat-up line of the night: "Can I buy you a drink. I thought your set was on fire, like my pants." Worst: "Hey, you look like an uglier Kate Moss. Want a drink?" Now, let me see, hmmm, no thanks, I'd rather eat my own toe cheese. . .

The taxi queue was massive 'cos it was chucking-out time. I lurked under a sex shop sign, leaning against the pole in what I hoped wasn't an "I'm pissed and only charge a fiver" kind of way. "You will call that guy, won't you?" Matt said, all concerned, wandering over to me.

"Yeah, yeah." He was looking at me really hard – where was everyone else? They were in the queue. Why did I have that last tequila? *Why?*

"I thought you were brilliant tonight. And this could really be something, you know. So many Ibiza legends start off in bars and get discovered by some big promoter. You should do a CD and send it off." He put his arm above my head and leaned on the pole too.

"Hmmm." Was he going to kiss me? Eeeeeeeek! My breath smelt of Zombies and tequila. Foulness. I swilled spit round and round in a frantic effort to get rid of it. Did I even want him to kiss me. . .? Where was Gemma? He fancied her. Oh God . . . I was imagining things as usual.

"Lilla, I know guys who wait years for this sort

of opportunity and now it's actually happening to you." He looked right in my eyes like he wanted to tell me I had a bogey poking out, or something.

"Hmmm." I couldn't speak 'cos I had a mouth full of spit. I had to swallow it, but it went down the wrong way and I choked.

"Bloody hell! Are you all right?" He slapped me across the back as I gasped for air. Gemma came stumbling over from the queue.

"Ooooh, Matt, you hero. Did you just stop her from choking on her own vomit?"

"Gemma! I was not being sick. I just, errmmmm, choked. That's all."

"Hmmm, on what?" she murmured, batting her lashes at Matt, who looked embarrassed. He deffo fancied her. Boys always got embarrassed when she was around.

"Come on, you three, we've got the girls a taxi!" Sol shouted and Gemma took Matt's hand and mine and dragged us along with her in the middle.

"Do you want to come back for coffee?" Gemma boldly asked Matt. "I'm sure Sol is."

"Naaah. I'm knackered. Next time."

I got in the car and wound down the windows.

"Gemma! Sol is *not* coming back for coffee. He's got work tomorrow." Sam looked indignant. Sol nodded in agreement. He was a gent anyway, I could tell. Sam would be bringing him back for "coffee" when she was ready. He did kiss her, though, and suddenly the pavement became fascinating for all of us.

"Call me!" Gemma shouted out to Matt.

He hadn't heard her and was looking at me. What? *What?* I *did* have a bogey, didn't I?

"When am I *ever* going to get a snog?" moaned Gemma as we pulled away. "I thought it was in the bag tonight."

"Gemma, give it a chance. We've only been here five minutes," Sam said.

"You've managed it!"

"Yes, what's going on with Sol?" I asked being nosy.

"Nothing. We're just having a laugh. I like him, and we're seeing each other on Thursday."

"Did you find out if you snogged him on Sunday?" asked Katie.

"Hmmm. It doesn't matter now. He took me outside for some fresh air earlier."

"And. . .?" Gemma pushed.

"And what?"

"What was he like out of ten?"

Sam didn't even hesitate: "Nine."

"Oooh – that's wet knickers!" Gemma laughed.

"Too much information!" Katie shouted.

"If that's a nine, what's a ten?" I wondered out loud.

"*No* knickers," Sam explained. "So hot they spontaneously combust!"

We'd arrived home. The kettle went on straight away. I had to have a coffee and toast. I fingered the business card. This was epic; I was going to call him later. What if he was joking, though, or made me do a trial in front of a panel of other DJs? What if—?

"JESUS! He's only fucking well coming out here!"

"Who? What?" I ran out of the kitchen, following Katie's voice down the corridor and into her bedroom. She was holding her mobile phone out so I could see the text message: *Hi Im trying to get a flight out – where u staying? Will call if I can get there. Lol Tom xx*

chapter

sixteen

"Now that's just psycho loon behaviour," Sam said when she saw the text. "It's like that film, with old wrinkle-dick in it, *Fatal Attraction*. We'll come home and find a gnome bubbling in a pot on the stove." We were lying on sunbeds drinking tea and crunching the toast I had managed to torch. The black sky was cracking round the edges, just starting to let the sun back into the world – the birds were going crazy. Yet again we saw in a new day.

"Thanks, Sam. Just what I need to hear." Katie put her head in her hands. "Just when he started not to be in my head so much, just when I thought I could get over him if I just never saw him, and he does this." She looked drained and teary.

"That's exactly what he wants you to be like. He won't even get a flight now, and all the fleapits will be booked up, he's got no chance," I reassured her. It really was a chance in a million.

We sat in silence for a bit, thinking about stuff. Katie was almost ready to kick sand in his face, but not just yet. I was falling asleep, the late nights catching up with me. We could talk more in the morning – if I could talk in the morning, my head was already starting to feel like a bass drum.

Later on that day I made the call. "Hi, is that Charlie? It's Lilla from last night in the U Bar." Lilla *who*?

"Hey. Now, when do you want to meet? I can see you tomorrow at three in the afternoon." Loud music in the background.

"Sure, that's fine." Eeeeek!

"We need to talk pay and sort out your hours and stuff like that. I'll go over our music policy –

all the usual guff." Like I knew what went on normally. "That's if you're still interested."

"Oh, I am!" Oooh, too eager beaver. He gave me directions and that was it – easy. I didn't have to bring my records or do a trial mix. This really was epic!

I fell asleep on a sunbed, under an umbrella luckily, when my phone woke me. "Philippa – where are you? We've been waiting half an hour!" Dad. I'd forgotten about lunch. Oops.

Lena had made a feast for the gods: aubergine dip, spicy seafood kebabs, potato salad, red onion and tomato salad, tuna steaks, garlic-marinated artichokes – no wonder Dad was marrying her, I would for food like this every night. We ate in the garden under the marquee umbrella that fitted snugly over the ginormous stone table, surrounded by basil plants and other herbs I hadn't a clue about.

"Your dad wanted to ask you something. Steve?" Lena gave him a Look. Oh, here we go. I wondered how long it would take before he got me in a headlock and told me I'd never make it as a DJ 'cos it took years of practice, dedication, talent, hard work—

"Aaah, yeah. Lena and I were wondering if you'd be bridesmaid at the wedding," he asked, all embarrassed. Now, I didn't see that coming. Cue awful dress, embarrassing photos, having to sit next to rellies I don't know who have bad breath *and* worse of all, getting to snog the best man – Dave! Aaaaaargh! Well, they do say the best weddings end in a fight. . .

"Erm. Sure. When is it?" I tried to smile but was convinced it came out as a grimace.

"You could be a bit more excited," Dad huffed.

"I am, it's just still a bit of a . . . er, you know, unexpected," I stammered. Well, come on, it was surreal, being bridesmaid at your own dad's wedding!

"It'll be at the end of September on the rooftop at Pacha after the closing parties," Lena gushed like a proper bride. "I know it's not a lot of time, but *OK* said they should be able to organize it, no problem."

"What? *OK*? *OK Magazine*? You didn't say I'd have to be in *OK Magazine*," I cried, panic gripping me. It would be soooooo embarrassing!

"What's wrong with *OK Magazine*?" Lena sniffed, raising a perfectly plucked eyebrow. "All the best people get their weddings in *OK*."

"Footballers' wives and soap stars have their weddings in *OK*," I blabbed blindly, not thinking what I was saying in my hungover state. "It'll look tacky."

Tumbleweed. . . I couldn't take the words back; they were hanging there smacking Lena in the face. I was expecting Dad to have a go any minute, but he didn't.

"Fine – you don't have to be a bridesmaid if that's the way you feel," she said icily. "Steve, haven't you got a niece who could do the job instead?" And she got up and started collecting plates, clunking them on top of one another and generally making a racket.

"Lena, love, Philippa didn't mean it, did you?" I did, I did!

Lena had gathered some dishes and stormed off into the kitchen before I could say sorry.

"What did you say that for?" Dad asked in a pained voice.

"I'm sorry – it just came out." I did feel bad now, 'cos she obviously loved all that *OK* bullshit.

"I'm going to get it in the neck now. She'll think I put you up to it."

"Why?"

"'Cos I said exactly the same thing a few days

ago. It looks like we're ganging up on her." This was all new to me – Dad actually caring about someone's feelings apart from his own. Or maybe he was worried all the nice food was about to disappear and he'd be back to Swedish air hostesses and ready meals.

I steeled myself for a grovelling apology and got up from the table. I had no idea how I was going to back-pedal out of this one. . .

"You're going to be in *OK Magazine*?!" Sam wet herself. "You who hates all that twaddle they use to describe fat celebs: sensual curves instead of rolls of flab? Ha ha ha ha ha. . ." Etc times a million. "Wait till the others hear this." Katie and Gemma had zipped to the shop to get supplies. Sam was floating in the pool awaiting their return. I don't think any of them had eaten since breakfast and it was now four.

Gemma was actually excited! "OHMIGOD! You're going to be a celebrity."

"No I'm not. I'm just going to wear a shit dress and carry a bunch of flowers."

"But you can have any dress you like if *OK* are paying, surely?" Katie said.

"Apparently it has to be along the theme of the

wedding, and the theme is green. It'll make me look like a corpse."

"Not if you get the right tone," Katie said.

I brought them up to date on the afternoon's row. "I got the impression Dad would have been happy with a few sausage rolls and some ham sarnies, but Lena wanted the biggest bash Ibiza had ever seen."

I had grovelled, saying I hadn't meant it, that I knew the wedding wouldn't be like a footballer's wife's wedding and that the rooftop at Pacha was a classy venue – not that I had a clue, having never been there. Lena eventually came round but not until she'd made it clear she thought I was a brat. Great. When she'd decided to forgive me, the magazines came out and I'd played along, oohing and ahhing over bridesmaids' dresses. I was going to look a tit in the national press – I bet she'd make me wear a meringue as revenge for my snidey comments.

To cap off the lunch, Dad started nosing around my DJing, asking questions – was I serious, was it just a hobby, had I done a demo CD, did I know a lot of promoters were sharks and coke-heads etc, blah? I tuned out – he was being patronizing, acting like I knew nothing, probably thinking I couldn't even put a record on a spindle. He then got in a huff when I refused to be baited and talk about it. I didn't want him to know a thing. This was my life, not his. . .

chapter
seventeen

Bar Lorca was where we'd eaten on our first day (I only realized when I turned up) and it seemed a bit shabby, squeezed between glamorous Code – a sleek, Italian-looking bar with the usual rich clientele and flash-looking interior – and a corner café selling club tickets and coffees. Propped up outside was a sign in the shape of a flamenco dancer holding a tray of food and drinks, and printed on her dress were the cocktails and food menus. There were a couple smoking fags and drinking beers on chairs outside, as well as a family eating a million and one different dishes including something that looked like starfish – eurgh. It did have a funky flashing sign emblazoned across the façade above the double door but obviously it wasn't switched on yet.

I walked in and the minute my eyes had adjusted from the bright sunlight outside I noticed Charlie sat at the bar talking to the barman. It was nicer inside, with dark wood floors and the obligatory comfy sofas with low tables so you could scoff tapas. Lights set in alcoves would be switched on when it got dark, and there were trendy black-and-white Ibiza photos on the walls in chunky wood frames. The decks were on a chrome console to the right of the bar, with more seating and a space for dancing should you so wish. It was more of a pre-club drinking venue than a getting down and boogying place like the U Bar.

"Hi! Lilla, glad you came." He shook my hand. "Can I get you a drink?" I had a beer and was introduced to Carlos as the new DJ! Ha ha ha ha ha. "Now, the music we play here's funky house – nothing too hard 'cos we don't want to put people off drinking. Punters come here before they go to El Divino or Pacha at about one or two, so they want to get in the mood, not peak too early, so keep it nice and light. We're open till three and I thought you could go on at nine."

I nodded. I knew I wouldn't get the glory hour, I was warm-up woman for whoever was the resident on those particular nights. I didn't care, I was going to be doing it for real, no bedroom, no pretending. "Money – we pay a hundred Euros per night for warm-up, but I want you to just do an hour first, as a sort of try-out, so you'll only get thirty." I just nodded dumbly, not even believing I was getting paid for doing this. Shouldn't I be paying him? "Now, any questions?"

"When do you want me to start?"

"Tonight." Fuckitydoody. Now where were my water wings? I believe you can drown at the deep end. . .

"Tonight!" Sam exclaimed. "I'm ringing Sol, we're coming to see you instead of going to DC10."

"No, Sam. You really want to see the Cuban Brothers. I'm only on for an hour."

"We can go later – you can come too, no big."

We were sat at a high table outside the Base Bar overlooking the Marina, the other end from Bar Lorca. "Will you need to buy some new records if you have to tone it down a bit?" Gemma asked playing with the straw in her Tequila Sunrise.

"Shit, I hadn't thought about it – yes, I will." Well done, Gemma!

Fast-forward ten minutes later, we walked into Slinky Records. Gemma charged straight up to the counter where Matt was ticking off something on a long invoice. "We have a very urgent request!" She got his attention. Aha – not really *well done* at all, just any excuse to see Matt.

"Hey, girls – what can I do?" He grinned at us all, eyes crinkling. Sol came over and winked at Sam.

"We need to get this superstar DJ some records, she's playing tonight!"

"Nice one, Lilla. At Bar Lorca?" Sol was impressed.

"Yeah, I've only got the warm-up slot and tonight is only a trial for an hour, but I need some more funky house, stuff that's not too hectic."

"Leave it with me." And Matt flipped the counter up and joined us in the shop. He started grabbing records from all over the place, not just out of their pigeonholes. "Some of that stuff you bought the other day will be perfect, but try these too," and he handed me the pile. I started the decks spinning and the shop just blurred into the background. Matt kept feeding me more and more tracks. In the end, he just stood there while I rushed through them. Then: "I can't remember what this one sounds like, can I have the other ear?" And we stood huddled under the phones, me pressed right up against him while he listened at the same time as me. But I couldn't hear the music, all I was aware of was his heart pressed into my shoulder and his soft breathing. He smelled of washing powder and something else, some deeply sexy aftershave. I felt this kind of tingling starting in the pit of my stomach, or maybe it was lower(!) and it spread like fire through my chest and up to my face. I hoped he couldn't feel my heart 'cos it was tap-dancing like a demented squirrel.

He took the cans off. "I think that one's great – it would go really well with that tune there," and he pointed to the next one on the pile. Huh? I couldn't speak. What was wrong with me? I had beads of sweat running down my sides. Foulness! He looked at me and smiled. "What time are you on?"

"Nine." I was struck down with monosyllabic lockjaw.

"Well, I'll pop in and say hi."

"No!" I squeaked before I knew what I was saying.

"Lilla! Why can't he come?" Gemma had sidled up without either of us noticing.

"Errr, he'll be . . . get bored. It's just us girls."

"Nonsense. Sol's coming. You can be my date." Gemma fluttered her eyelashes at him.

He looked at me to see what I'd say. "If you're sure, Lilla?"

"Course she's sure, she's just nervous about tonight, aren't you?" Gemma grinned at me.

"Yeah, sorry. Come along." I was gonna kill her. I'd never concentrate if he was there – I'd fluff it.

"No worries. Try that tune though. See you later." And he sauntered off back to the counter where Sam was chatting to Sol. Why couldn't I ever say the right thing? Why was I such a dweeb?

"I've got a date!" Gemma crowed as we left the shop. "Matt's coming with me tonight to Bar Lorca. This is it, I'm finally going to get my man!" She rubbed her hands, obviously planning the outfit to snare him properly.

We were walking back to the bikes and I suddenly felt a sledgehammer hit me in the stomach. I was jealous. I was jealous that Matt was going with Gemma. Why did I have to fancy him now? Anyway, it didn't matter, he'd liked her from the start and there was no way I could compete with Gemma – look at her!

"Wow!" Sam said. "So, did he ask you out?"

"Not exactly, I asked him," she admitted. "I have to say, I was just about to give up, 'cos I thought he liked Lilla, but he said yes." She looked at me then. "You don't mind me bringing him tonight, do you?" she asked, remembering my outburst.

"Don't be silly, you go for it. He obviously likes you." What else could I say?

"You would say if you liked him, though, wouldn't you?" she probed.

"Gemma! I don't fancy him!" This satisfied her and she smiled, linking arms with me all the way to the bikes. Why did I just do that? I fancied him so much it hurt. Bollocks. I'd just have to ignore him all night and get over it. Not that easy when he gives me sweaty palms!

I couldn't eat any dinner; I just practised and practised when we got in, playing all the tunes, getting to know them. Katie rang Andy and told him about my debut, and he asked if he could bring some mates before he went off to work. There would be quite a crowd there. Better than an empty bar, I suppose.

Gemma made cocktails before we left; I downed mine in one go. "Steady on, Lils, you won't be able to see the decks," Sam laughed. I decided to wear something low-key. So grey combats, tight red laced-up T and trainers was my chosen uniform, with a little make-up.

Bar Lorca's sign was lit up when we got there at half eight. It wasn't yet dark but it instantly made it look a lot groovier. People were sat outside and in. It wasn't heaving, but it wasn't empty either. Carlos was behind the bar with a blonde Australian girl called Kelly. I had a butterfly farm fluttering my tummy. "Is Charlie in?" I asked her. He was out the back and she pointed to a door somewhere by the loos that was marked Private. Carlos smiled, "Good luck for tonight."

I knocked. "It's Lilla!"

"Come in." He was sat behind a desk in a dingy broom cupboard of a room with another surfer-dude guy sitting on a bashed-up filing cabinet to the right. Piles of empty beer crates threatened to topple over on to him.

"All set for tonight?" He looked a bit stary and mad.

"Yep, bought some new tunes. Can you show me the mixer and stuff?"

"Sure. Just a sec." Surfer Dude offered him a rolled up note, and that's when I clocked the chopped-up lines of white powder on the desk. Oh foulness, he was a cliché!

chapter

eighteen

"Want a line?" So, Surfer Dude *could* speak.

"No thanks," I replied in what I hoped wasn't my schoolteacher's voice. Charlie (oh, how that name suited him now) pinched his nose then sniffed furiously. I'd never actually seen anyone snort it before (now I knew why). Even though my dad was addicted for years, he kept it hidden from me. Surfer shrugged and bent over the table. I turned away — it looked so desperate and unattractive. It was absolutely gross.

"Right, let's go." I was propelled through the door and back outside where the others were waiting with my record bag. I should have asked him to show me earlier, but forgot. Duuuur. It was all pretty easy anyway; I could have worked it out myself. "Whenever you're ready, Lilla." A Spanish house CD was playing in the meantime. The girls had sat down opposite at a table. The boys hadn't rocked up yet. Good, it meant I could get used to the set-up without them witnessing any major clangers.

It was like messing about in Katie's bedroom, 'cos no one was going to dance, just listen. I could almost relax and forget about people, though my fingers were shaking as I put the needle on the first record, and my sweat glands were on overdrive under my arms. How attractive. After twenty minutes, another beer appeared at my elbow – Andy brought it over. "Doing great, lady." He kissed me on the cheek.

Outside was much busier now and waiters were running backwards and forwards with drinks and tapas. Sol and Matt were here, sat with the girls, as well as Andy and some of his friends from Pacha. When I gazed at Matt I felt sick – he looked gorgeous in a black short-sleeved shirt and jeans.

He'd really made an effort for Gemma tonight, and she looked amazing as usual. Just as I was staring at him, he glanced up and caught me. Oh, the shame. I could feel my cheeks explode as I busily bent down and shuffled through my record box.

Charlie kept behind the bar, making cocktails with Carlos and Kelly and chatting up the customers. My new tunes were excellent, even if I do say so myself. When I next checked the room, Gemma was on one barstool and Charlie was on the other, I couldn't see his face, but Gemma's was showing green light for go. So fickle – what about Matt and the Date? I searched for him through the crowd and he was too busy laughing with Andy to even notice.

Time flew and before I knew it, my last record was playing. Enrique the usual guy was waiting behind me, scowling. He was brusque, obviously not impressed a girl was DJing before him. Whatever. I hoped Charlie thought my tunes were OK. I sat down with the others, records at my feet – it was all a bit of an anticlimax. I couldn't put my finger on why, but it wasn't as good as the other night. Gemma bounded over. "You were amazing! Charlie thought you were superb – he said so. I think you needn't worry about the trial."

Why that annoyed me, I had no idea. Why couldn't she let him tell me himself? What did she know about what was good and what wasn't? Get me – someone give me a ladder so I could get over myself! Something was nipping me in the tummy and making it flare up so I felt grouchy. Everyone else cooed at me as well, but it didn't matter till Charlie had said it. I was on edge – maybe he'd changed his mind.

Five minutes after I'd finished, he sauntered over with a beer, for me it turned out, and my pay. "Lilla, you were fantastic. Just what I was looking for, the right mix of funky and tribal. So, can you do a full shift next Tuesday, starting at nine again? We'll give it a while and then see about moving you to other more popular nights." She shoots, she scores! She gets to stay the whole summer and work. . .

"Just one thing, would you mind wearing something a little more glam next time?" What?!!!!! "Something more like your friend Gemma here wears?" In case you're wondering: the Old Faithful crowd-puller – the boob tube and tighter than skin spray-on denim hipsters with killah heels, massive grin.

"Sure." Fume, fume, fume. Sam stared at me, but kept her opinions closely zipped up.

"Excellent. See you next week then." And he disappeared back to the bar where a few ladies had gathered, anxiously awaiting his return.

"I can't believe you let him speak to you like that!" Sam exploded.

"Why? He's selling a night. The people who work for him have to look good!" Gemma replied.

"Gee, thanks, Gem. I had no idea I looked a state. I'd rather dress like this than like a hooker." That was a bit mean. . .

"Ooooooh! Handbags at dawn!" Andy cried in his campest voice.

She looked at me with raised eyebrows, then whistled through her teeth, a sign that she thought I'd gone too far. Any minute now she'd hit me with a verbal missile, but she didn't. "I'm going to the bar. Does anyone want a drink?" she asked instead. "Matt, can you help me carry them?" she asked sweetly and picked her way to the bar.

Andy stood up to let Matt past and made an announcement: "We've got to scoot to work but I'm going to put all your names on the VIP list for tonight, so please come, should be a laugh." His mates all stood up too and said byes to everyone. "All drinks'll be free, so don't worry about your budget, ladies." He knew we were going to be selling our bodies by the end of next week if we didn't rein ourselves in. Looked like I would be ringing Lena and asking for free entry to all the clubs after all. Much as I was loath to, especially after yesterday's fiasco. "Just ask for me when you get there and I'll take you through."

Gem, Katie and I were planning on going home tonight after my set 'cos we were knackered and piss-poor, but VIP to Pacha? Sam and Sol decided to blow out the naked break-dancing Cuban Brothers and come with us. They could see them another time. Gem had scammed a round of tequila shots from Charlie – looked like we were going to be seeing in another dawn after all. Shit – my liver was packing its bags and going on holiday. . .

Pacha – welcome to the land of the bold and the beautiful, all ages catered for. "It's like a pop video!" Katie said in awe as we stood in the foyer (plants, plants and more plants) waiting for the others. The outside was illuminated, coloured filters bouncing off the white plaster walls and palms as people queued to get in – we didn't have to! Stunning women wandered past, heels like skyscrapers, hair down to their waists. "Hookers,"

Andy whispered. Katie's hand flew up to her mouth in disbelief. "Wait till you get to VIP, you be careful — the men in there are like vultures! But you won't have to pay for a thing!"

Once we were all rounded up Andy took us through a room to the right of the foyer and round the back way through some double doors. It was a rabbit warren — strip lighting overhead, highlighting the bags under my eyes nicely. Andy was scurrying like the white rabbit from *Alice in Wonderland*. He was dressed in a sailor outfit, orange make-up on, tight white vest, his hair slicked back under his hat. "I'm with the mermaid tonight!" was his explanation. We would have to wait and see.

We passed Spanish waiters sitting on crates of beer smoking fags, staring at us insolently. We charged through what looked like a kitchen area, people shouting in Spanish and English, pans crashing, twisting and turning past stacks of vodka bottles and other assorted beverages. It was hard to keep up with Andy and I was glad of my trainers. Gemma was slipping and sliding, holding on to Matt so she didn't go arse over tit. Suddenly we were plunged into darkness through another set of doors — we were in VIP.

Andy was standing by a table marked "Reserved". "This is for you guys, and ladies, I've got to dash – have a wicked night, might see you later," and he kissed us all, disappearing through the doors from which we had appeared. We sat down in a daze and drank it all in. Our table was at the back of the middle tier – the whole area was on different levels, overlooked above by a mezzanine bar area with railings to stop people falling in here. Down to the front was the DJ booth, a small area in front of it roped off, to stop us hassling the gods, I assumed.

"Isn't that Roger Sanchez playing?" asked Gemma. Wow! I could just about see him, hands in the air to the crowd below on the immense ocean of a dance floor surrounding us. He was like Jesus preaching to the masses. I stood up and looked over the railing on to the dance floor – sparkly gorgeous girls in bikini tops and shorts writhed on podiums to the right of it, enormous palms towered above, their frondy leaves catching the disco lights. Steps from the bar area above us twisted down like a Cinderella staircase to a mini stage area rammed with clubbers gyrating like loons. The place was crammed to capacity, or so it seemed. We would need to go and explore 'cos we couldn't see it all from here.

"This place is so sophisticated. I love it!" Katie gushed.

Other tables were packed as well. Down below lounged loads of older guys, Peter Stringfellow types, with pretty girls wedged in between them, champagne flowing. "This place is mental," Matt shouted above the music. "I've never been in the VIP before. Did you see that guy that used to go out with Kylie – he's at one of the tables down there." I stretched my neck to see and sure enough, there he was, surrounded by girls, two of whom were the hookers Andy had pointed out earlier. As soon as I'd spotted him, I noticed two actresses from a dodgy soap back home on a table behind that one. It was all rather surreal.

"Does anyone want to go and dance?" I asked hopefully.

"Can we stay and get some drinks first?' Gemma asked. "Andy gave me some free drinks tickets. It's not often that we get into VIP, is it?" She had a point there.

The boys went to the bar with the tickets, leaving us on our own. "So, girls, I think I'll deffo score with Matt tonight!" Gemma said excitedly. "He's been so lovely all evening, telling me I look good and how glad he is that we all met up." She *really* did like him.

"Go for it," I said trying to sound enthusiastic.

"Don't worry, I will."

"Well, I've got some good news," said Katie, checking her phone after it vibrated in her pocket. "Bastard-features couldn't get a flight!"

"Oh, that's wicked!" Sam said. "What a relief."

"Yes, but he's decided to bombard me with really awful texts instead – I've had three all at once, informing me I am a bitch, I've ruined his life, hoping I fail my exams." She shook her head in disbelief. "I can't believe he's doing this."

I took her hand. "Ignore them. He's really fucked in the head. He just wants to ruin your time here, don't let him."

She nodded. "I never thought he would ever be this shitty. Just goes to show you think you know someone. . ." None of this surprised me at all, but I wasn't going to start up that old record again.

"Excuse me, ladies," an American voice drawled. We looked round. Standing there was a good-looking guy in his mid twenties, dressed in combats and T, but looking like he should have been in a suit. "My friends and I were wondering whether you'd finished with your gentlemen and would like to join us instead?"

I choked on my chewing gum. He thought we were hookers!

chapter
nineteen

Gemma was quick off the mark. "We'll have to think about it, but how about you get us a bottle of Cristal while we do?" And she smiled in such a demure way that even I thought she was an angel.

"It would be my pleasure." Off he went to his table, rubbing his hands.

"Gemma! Now they really will think we're prostitutes!" Katie cried.

"So what! We may as well fleece them if they're that stupid. We're with the boys and they can't do anything or we'll call security!" She giggled. "We can do this all night. Andy was right, we won't have to pay for anything."

"But how did you even know what to ask for?" Sam was flabbergasted.

"Cristal is what P Diddy always drinks at those parties in *Heat* magazine."

"But what is it?" I asked.

"Only the most expensive champagne there is!" said Katie, pointing at the drinks menu. "Four hundred Euros a bottle!"

A red sign flashed in my mind: no such thing as a free lunch. "Just stay out of their way if they give it to us," I said. Sure enough, just as the boys came back with a round of beers, along came the silver bucket. Well, it was a shame to waste it.

Three am, and we'd all been dancing non-stop for about two hours on the main floor below VIP. Andy appeared on a mobile stage in the middle of the dance floor with two other guys, all dressed as sailors, writhing round a mermaid — it was excellent. An MC was rapping over the top of some funked-up tune and we were all going mental, bouncing up and down. I looked over to Gemma just in time to see her lunge at Matt and snog him full on. We all pretended not to see, but it was hard to miss, she was eating him alive! He didn't look like he was complaining, though.

I rolled my eyes. I'd known that this was bound to happen at some point, but it didn't make it any easier. Suddenly I wanted to go home. My legs were hurting, we'd run out of drinks tickets and I was sick of telling drunken boys to piss off and leave me alone. Everyone else was having a wicked time – Katie was dancing like a pop pixie, surrounded by boys and carrying off the "look but don't touch" vibe really well. Her gang of admirers all kept a respectful distance and if they got too close, she gave them a Look.

I needed to go and have a word with myself and chill out so I slipped away to VIP. Our table was still reserved and I plonked myself down – head in my hands. "Can I get you a drink?" A cute waiter was standing next to the table. I ordered a vodka and sat in a daze, waiting for it to arrive, vowing that by the time I'd finished it, I would have snapped out of this mood and be able to go and dance like a loon. Even if Gemma was still snogging Matt. My vodka turned up and I scrabbled around for money, realizing Katie had it in her purse.

"I don't have any money."

"Put it on our bill." It was the smooth American. My tummy tightened. I had to accept or the waiter would go mad. Why was my life such a drama?

"Thank you. You don't have to."

"I can't leave a lady in distress," he smarmed. "Join our table, I notice you're on your own."

"My friends will be back in a bit, I'm going to wait here."

"*My* friends all want to meet *you*. We've got another bottle of Cristal on the go – your favourite, I believe." Oh, how could I resist, especially when he winked.

"Honestly, my boyfriend will wonder where I am if he comes up here." His face froze.

"Fine. If you change your mind." And he sloped off to his table, shrugging his shoulders. I necked my vodka; I was outta here the minute I'd had a wee. Mr Sanchez moved the music up a gear – I was ready to go back down and be a lot more chilled and go with the flow. *Matt?* Matt who?

The loos in VIP were unisex and I came out of my cubicle to find American Guy standing outside mine.

"We really should stop meeting like this." Oh fuckit. . .

"Yes, we should, so I'm leaving."

He reached his hand out to stop me. "What if we *paid* you to stay?"

"What? Why?"

"We like you. You're not like the other *girls* that work here. You look sweet." Oh thank you, like that's a compliment coming from you, LOSER.

"I don't work here! I'm not a hooker, you fuckwit." I pushed past him but he grabbed my arm as I stormed past.

"Hey, hey, what's the rush? At least share a line with me, honey." He looked like Charlie had done earlier and it made sense now why he was being such a dick. These guys were no advert for taking drugs. I felt a tiny panic fairy start fluttering. Why me?

"Lilla, are you OK?" Matt was at the loo door. Let the credits roll for cheesy damsel in distress silent movie. What was I, tied to a railway track or something?

"Nice to meet you," American Guy said, and made a sharp exit – so much for the movie villain. What was it with coke-heads? They thought they ruled the universe.

"As usual I was getting into trouble."

Matt stepped closer to me. "What are we going to do with you? You need a minder." And he touched my face gently, air getting strangled in my throat, his eyes searching out mine. I could feel his warm breath on my nose and he stroked my hair, letting his hand fall down my neck and trace a line to that soft bit at the base of my throat where my pulse raced just under the skin. My pants were on fire – no, my pants had disintegrated, and he hadn't even kissed me, yet. Was he going to? Oh, God, I really wanted him to. I was evil, he was with Gemma. . .

"You need to stop getting into trouble," he whispered, just before he touched his nose to mine and looked right in my head. Boy, did I want to find out what fourth base was like there and then, in a loo cubicle if necessary. Any romantic thoughts of being deflowered in a field on a picnic blanket were fleeing from my brain. Lust was definitely making a takeover bid for all my sexual fantasies.

"Matt."

"Yes?"

"What about Gemma?"

"What about her?"

"I thought you—" But I didn't finish 'cos next thing I knew he was kissing me. His lips were like velvet and he nibbled my bottom lip, darting his tongue into my mouth, finding mine and pressing so gently that I wanted to rip his clothes off. My hands found themselves wrapped round his head, pulling him into me, playing with his hair. I had never ever felt this turned on before, ever! A definite eleven on the scale.

He lifted his head and looked at me. "I have wanted to do that from the minute I saw you."

I took my arms down from his neck and stepped back, instantly feeling hideously guilty. "I can't do this. Gemma really likes you."

"Lilla! God, you're embarrassing!" Gemma was standing there, how long she'd been hovering, I had no idea. "I'm sorry, Matt. I didn't know Lilla was giving you a rundown of how I felt." She was smiling in an awkward manner, looking very pissed, eyes like slits. She'd only heard the last bit – phew.

"Gemma! I wasn't telling him, it's just that, well, I er. . ." What could I say? I've spent the last week in denial, that I fancy Matt as much as you do? Why was life like poo on a stick sometimes?

"Gemma, let's go back to the dance floor. People will think we're having a party in here." I took her elbow and manoeuvred her out of the loo. Matt touched my bum and I turned round. He shook his head in a "what is going on?" way.

I stopped and he grabbed me and kissed me again while Gemma was walking out of VIP. I could have stayed in that loo all night and locked the door. "We haven't finished," he said.

"No, we have." I pulled away, an ache of unspent energy in my groin!

"Why? She's so wasted she won't give a toss."

"No, but I do, she's my friend. And you did kiss her earlier!"

"She kissed me! I couldn't get away!"

"Don't give me that. You came as her date tonight." I looked at him. "You led her on, she thinks you like her."

"I've never made out tonight was a 'date'. Anyway, I thought you didn't like me! You ran away just as I was going to ask you out the other day, what else was I supposed to think?"

"I can explain, but now isn't the time." I opened the loo door. This was getting a bit too *Dawson's Creek*.

"Explain now." His voice was breathless and I couldn't help myself, honest – I had to kiss him again, just once before we went outside. We were standing in the loo door, for everyone to see and I just didn't care. All I wanted was him to never stop.

"Lilla, I —" Gemma had stumbled back to see where I was. "Oh!"

I didn't know what to do. She was standing there looking at us, her mouth opening and closing, and then she turned and scooted off as fast as her drunken legs could carry her.

chapter

twenty

I ran after her, leaving Matt. Oh, God, she was going to kill me. I never did stuff like this. "Gemma! Gemma, come back!" She was just ahead of me in the foyer, heading up some stairs. I caught up with her. "Look, I'm really sorry, I truly am. I don't know what to say to make it better."

She turned round on the stairs and stopped. People were pushing past us to get to the roof terrace. "I don't understand you, Lilla. You said you didn't like him."

"I know."

"So why were you snogging him in the loo?" she slurred. "That's pretty fucking sneaky!"

I just looked at her, unable to give an excuse — there wasn't one. I shrugged, knowing I was being lame.

"Do you know what I think?" she asked. I shook my head. "I think he liked you all along and only said yes tonight so he could see you."

I stared at the steps, avoiding her gaze. She should have been battering me with her handbag by now, if she'd had one. "I've never had to try so hard with a guy in my life — it makes sense now. He's not even all that. . ."

I looked up. "He kissed me first, Gem. I promise I didn't run after him."

"You could have said no, you cow!" Because she was so drunk I couldn't tell if she was really angry or just mildly pissed off.

"I did, at first, but he was persistent. . ."

"Hmmm. . . Do you like him?"

"Yes. A lot." I was waiting for some sort of tantrum.

"You owe me, big time, Philippa Wheeler. I want a massive grovelling drink from you, in fact, I want a champagne cocktail." She motioned me to go down the steps and as I turned round she flicked my ear. "Oh, sorry, did that hurt?"

"Ow! Yes!" I looked back at her.

She stuck out her tongue and then smirked. "Sloppy seconds ain't my style anyhow," she said and shoved me in the direction of the dance floor.

We pulled up outside the gate in a taxi. "Wow, this place is pretty cool!" Sol whistled as Matt paid the driver. Usually I would be starving, eager to get the toast on and make a cuppa, but I felt too nervous and jumpy. After Gemma and I had had our little tête-à-tête on the stairs, she'd gone into Operation Get A Snog overdrive. The others had no idea what had happened between Matt and me, and I was beginning to wonder if it had happened at all now 'cos for the rest of the night he didn't try and kiss me again. Oh, he was there, dancing right behind me, sending sparks up my spine, but he wouldn't actually touch me and there was no way I was going to make a move in front of everyone, if at all.

Gemma found a boy in the same time I need to take my make-up off after a night out. One minute she was pole-dancing, the next she was attached like a leech to some guy's face, pressed up against a pillar. When we decided to call it a night, she wanted to stay and see in the morning with him (Alex, I think his name was, good-looking, black hair, chiselled jaw). I said we should let her, but Sam was having none of it. "What if he's an axe murderer? We can't let her go with him." So a spat ensued, Sam trying to force Gemma to come back and Gemma determined to stay. She was soooo drunk and even though this guy was nice, you just never knew. So he came back with us, and the minute we got in the villa they headed to her room and didn't come out again till the next day.

It was just getting light and we were sat by the pool, sipping tea and listening to chill-out tunes. I pushed my toast round my plate, my tummy in knots. I couldn't bear this, sitting next to Matt on a sunbed, our knees touching, but not speaking. Katie, Sam and Sol were laughing about something from the evening.

"I'm going to bed, night," I said and just walked into the house, looking back at Matt who was staring at me. It was a gamble. I lay on the bed buzzing, hoping he'd come, and about two minutes later there was a knock on my door.

"Can I come in?" Of course he could! He sat on the edge of the bed gazing at me. I could feel my heart banging in my ribcage, making the bed vibrate. "So, is it safe to be in here? I'm not going to get told off?"

I laughed nervously. "I think Gemma's a bit distracted now. . ."

He lay down next to me. "Good." His breathing was shallow, matching mine. "Can I do this?" And he stroked my hair, looking all the time into my eyes.

"Yes," I breathed, my chest heaving up and down.

"Can I do this?" He pecked me on the nose. He knew how to tease!

"You already did."

"How about this?" He leaned right over and kissed me properly on the mouth, prising me open like an oyster so I automatically responded, wrapping my arms around his neck, pulling him on top of me, feeling how horny he was. This time I knew I didn't have to stop.

He took his time, treating me like a fragile piece of china that might crack. I didn't care if tonight was never repeated, if this really was just a one-night stand, though I felt it wasn't. He was so kind and sexy and considerate that it felt right. Better than with Dan who I had been going out with for a few months. Fumbling behind the bike sheds with him wasn't even comparable to this.

Matt expertly slid on a condom, then sensed my nerves twitching. "What's the matter, Lilla?"

I must have looked like a frightened rabbit. "I'm . . . er . . . I haven't really done this. . ." I trailed off, not wanting to admit my inexperience fully. My face burned.

"Do you want me to stop?" He came and lay down beside me. "I'll do whatever you want me to." He stroked my hair again.

"No, I just wanted you to know." I couldn't stop now. I would explode all over the bed! I needed to feel him inside me.

"Sure? I won't hurt you, I promise, and if I do, tell me to stop. This isn't a test you have to pass, we have all the time in the world, well, till I have to go to work!" He kissed me and it made me want him even more, so I wrapped my legs round him and slid my hand down, gently nudging him towards me.

As he pushed tentatively inside, he gasped, moving ever so slowly, "Are you OK?"

I couldn't reply; I had never felt so open before. I just nodded, pushing up against him, wanting him further inside, but that hurt and I clenched my teeth.

"Take it slowly, sweetheart, it isn't a race." And he kissed my eyelids and pulled out a bit. The more he moved, the more I wanted him further, but he knew when and how. I could hear someone moaning, then clocked it was me! Oh, hello, porn actress, anyone? He was nibbling my neck and our movements were getting a lot more urgent, though he was careful not to hurt me. "Lilla, sweetheart, I think I'm going to come, how close are you?" Now, isn't that a bit like asking a blind person if they like the view?

"I don't know." All I knew was that I didn't want him to stop moving 'cos I felt like something was going to happen, but wasn't quite sure what. He stopped and pressed down on me, moving much more slowly. That was it, I was all over the place, scratching his back, arching upwards until I could feel a warm sneeze build up in my tummy, and spread between my legs – my knees were jelly. At the same time he shook, suddenly pushing really hard inside me, making me shout out in pain. Something was busily going mental inside me, like I was having a bad attack of cramp, but it was delicious all at the same time.

My head stood still, cheeks aflame and Matt was buried in my neck, breathing deeply. "I'm *so* sorry, I hurt you, didn't I?"

I lifted his chin, to face me – he looked embarrassed. "Don't be silly. God, that was amazing."

"Lilla, you don't know how amazing *you* were. I've never been that turned on before." The bullshit detector's batteries had run out, but my gut instinct told me he wasn't feeding me a line.

"Me neither. Not ever, it even beat playing at Space with Fatboy Slim as my warm-up guy." He laughed and kissed my face all over, starting with my eyebrows and working his way to my lips. Now I knew what all the fuss was about. . .

"Afternoon!" Sam shouted from her sunbed as I crept out to the pool, hoping everyone else was in bed. It was about one. Gemma was still nowhere to be seen. I didn't feel too bad considering I'd only had about an hour's sleep. I sat down underneath the vines; the sun was going to be too much for me right now.

"What time did Matt leave?" Katie asked walking up behind me, yawning and clutching a cup of tea. So they all knew then, it wasn't hard to work out. . .

"About eleven – he had to get back for work."

"He must have left with Sol," Sam said.

"So what happened?" Katie asked me.

"Nothing." Which wasn't strictly true. Everything had happened, it was hnnnnggggg. . .

"Really? You didn't even kiss him?" Sam asked, knowing full well I was covering up.

"Well, yes, I did, but not just then, at the club too."

"WHAT? When? I didn't know!" Katie cried. "You have to tell us now, it's not fair."

So I told them. . .

"OHMIGOD! So you did it?" Katie gasped when I'd finished. "And it was earth-shattering? Wow. . ." Obviously I didn't go into that much detail, just the bare essentials.

"We did it more than once, actually – two more times before he went to work at eleven."

"And you came each time?" Sam asked, unbelieving.

"Hmmmyeah." The last time had been pretty spectacular. I'd felt like my whole body was melting into his. "Poor Matt, he has to be at work and he's had no sleep whatsoever."

His kiss as he left was intense. "Lilla, this isn't just for now. I mean, I *will* see you again, if you want to, that is. . ."

"What do you think?" I'd teased. "I might be

busy for the rest of the summer, I mean, what if I have to wash my hair every night?"

"So, you're an item?" Sam asked.

"I don't know, we'll see." I didn't want to start thinking like that, that's when it gets messy. Go with the flow, I always think.

"Has Gemma not got up yet?" I asked.

"Nope. Alex left after Matt and Sol – I heard her door go. I checked she was still alive, before you ask!"

"I guess she got her snog then!" I said, and we all burst out laughing.

"D'you think she'll see him again?" Katie asked.

"What do *you* think?" Sam said sarcastically. "This is Gemma we're talking about."

"So, you and Sol," Katie probed Sam, changing the subject, "he's keen!"

"Hmmmmmaybe," Sam mumbled, not comfortable being under the spotlight.

"Of course he is, he stayed the night!" Katie said.

"I don't know, Katie. I'm no good at this part," she sighed, fiddling with her lip balm. "I'm better at keeping things casual. I'm just not used to seeing someone, hoping they'll call, and now he's seen me, you know, naked, it's worse."

I knew what she meant, but there was no point worrying about it or you'd never go out with anyone or leave the house ever again. But then I wasn't a complete control freak like Sam. Honestly, I'm not. I couldn't care if Matt never called, not for a second. I only had my phone next to me in case Dad called, really!

chapter
twenty-one

On Monday I'd woken up really early to go for a pee, opened my door and screamed my head off. Well, wouldn't you freak faced with a sea of squidgy noses and wonky eyes all looking at you naked? An army of gnomes were squatting outside my room holding up "Happy Birthday, Lilla!" on bits of paper. I swear our villa is possessed by a poltergeist. They were like those rocks in the Arizona desert, the ones that move in the night and no one knows how. . .

The girls had laid on a wonderful champoo brekkie, did me proud: warm croissants, pain au chocolat, smoked salmon, perfect poached eggs – the works. Mum called, got all tearful, her baby becoming a grown-up (how did she know about Matt?). She said I could have my present when I got home as it was too big to send out with Katie. Nice one! Best of all, surprisingly, was Dad and Lena arriving for breakfast, my embarrassing jibe about the wedding hopefully swept under a carpet somewhere. The girls knew they were coming and had hidden the decks, knowing I would have a fit if Dad saw them and started asking questions or having a go again. They turned up at ten bringing the champoo, a chocolate cake (baked by Lena) with eighteen candles, and my present: a Gucci watch! "Thanks, Dad!" That deserved a kiss. The girls had clubbed together and bought me some new tunes (always needed) and a spangly gold boob tube top.

"To my little girl, Philippa, now old enough to tell her old man where to go!" I'll drink to that, but luckily Dad stuck with orange juice. . .

Matt had called me in the morning, wishing me happy birthday. All weekend I'd had texts, and he called Sunday too. "He's keen!" Sam had said after his call as we all sat outside Café Del Mar, watching the fiery orange sun melt into the sea. "He wants you baaaad, girl." Oh yeah?

"Yeah, lucky cow. I tried so hard and it was you he fancied all along," Gemma had said, pretending to be in a sulk. "At least we know you're *not* a lesbian now."

In a stark contrast to my loved-up texts, Katie was still getting evil ones from Tom, stuck at home, determined to give her a hard time. "Thing is," she said, "it's water off a duck's back. I actually hate him now. I never realized how petty and small-minded he really is. Why didn't anyone tell me?"

"Like you would have listened!" I cried. "You worshipped him."

"Jeeeeeeeeeeeeez. Was I mad? What a lucky escape. . ."

The plan that evening was to go to Manumission, held at the club Privilege; Sol had managed to get us in on the guest list. Sam thought she would take us into San Antonio first (eeek!) to an amazingly cool bar Sol had told her about, but it meant we had to walk through the West End – BIG mistake. It's basically a strip of pulling bars and dodgy clubs that cater for English tourists – lager, lager, lager. It's what Mum thinks of when she thinks of Ibiza.

There are a few good places, but we ended up (by mistake) in the mingingest, munterville bar from hell. "Ladies, ladies, here, have these tickets, free drinks before eleven for beautiful ladies." "Girls, oh you lot are gorgeous, we need you inside, come on, I'll personally buy *you* a drink, treacle." "Oh, have I died and gone to heaven 'cos you girls look like angels, come in, free drinks for you ladies, just say Jason said so." "Can I marry you?" Argh!!!!!! Every joint we passed had an English tout outside, dragging people in off the street. Gullible girls thinking the guys actually *liked* them fell for the patter and were shepherded inside, giggling that Kevin/Gary/Jason/Phil/Antony fancied them. Durrrrr!! It was Blackpool with heating.

"I can't find where we're supposed to be going," Sam said puzzling over a bit of paper. "Shall we just go in there? There's no gross tout, so maybe it's OK." We were so fed up of the constant barrage and bum gropes that we tamely followed her inside.

It was bursting with punters, most of them downing the cheap watered-down shots.

"I'm not sure about this place." Katie Doubting Thomas again. "It feels odd – I mean, why is everything made of rubber, even the tables?"

"It'll be fine, we'll just have a few drinks and go back to the Old Town, or somewhere else." So we battled to the bar and ordered our shots. The music was so cheesy it was ripe and people were just dancing where they stood.

"You girls want a drink?" We had been in there exactly three minutes and he was a two on the scale: England shirt, baggy jeans (no bum – I checked), white trainers, skinhead and red face – just my type.

"No thanks, we just got one," Sam replied briskly.

"So? I wasn't actually going to *buy* you one, it's just a way to get the ball rolling, innit?" And he had the cheek to wink! "A drink can lead to other things, if you're lucky."

"Oh, you're a real charmer, aren't you?" Sam was on a roll. "I mean, that line's so good I think I might actually want to shag you, right now. Shall I meet you in the loo in five minutes, give me time to get my knickers off." She smiled, ironically, of course.

"You bitch, I was only being nice," he huffed.

"Yeah? Well, don't. I'd rather be a bitch than a walking dictionary of degrading one-liners and egocentric shite." He was baffled – long words were not part of his vocab.

"Fucking lesbian. . ." We were making friends fast.

Ten mingers later (I kid you not, we were like honey to them) and Gemma was giving the latest one the red card, the music went quiet and the DJ got on the mike. "Is everyone ready?" "Yes!" "I can't hear you, is everyone ready for the start of the party?" "YESSSSSS!!!"

"What's going on?" I shouted over the shrieking. Just as I said that, a horn blared out and everyone started screaming, and then it happened: foam pumped from above on to the floor and tables right in front of us.

"Run!" Sam yelled. We thought we'd missed it 'cos it was all happening behind us, but you try running in platforms – trainers, where are you when I need you?! We managed to push our way through packs of men, who tried to stop us, so Sam lamped one of them. Just before we reached the door, more foam sprayed everywhere and this time we ran straight into it.

"I can't see! My contact fell out!" Katie yelled and careered into a table full of blokes, all covered in foam, taking me down with her. My face landed in someone's crotch. "While you're down there, love!" Yeah, funny, ha ha. Gemma slipped over and

213

ripped her trousers up the bum crack revealing her cheeks. Sam did start laughing until she tripped on my leg sticking out from the guy's chair and flew out the door, landing in a heap. Stylish exit. Outside we must have looked a sight – make-up in muddy pools on our chests.

"You've got a white Afro!" Gemma squealed at me.

People were pointing at us in the street; we looked like extras from some oddball fifties sci-fi movie: *Escape from the Foam Monster*. All our clothes were completely ruined. The dye from Sam's dark blue lace-up top was running down her arms.

"So, who wins the wet T-shirt competition?" Sam asked. We looked at each other and burst out laughing – it had to be Katie. Her white chiffon top was completely see-through, her rosy pink nipples glaring out for all to see.

"Great, not only am I blind but I'm naked too. Please can we go before I get carted off to the circus?"

"Oi, love, nice raspberries! It's my mate's birthday – tenner for a lapdance?"

"No, it's fifty quid and he's too ugly!" Oh, San An, what a classy place, I just *wished* we'd discovered it sooner. . . Not.

"Sam, look! See the name of the bar?" I groaned, noticing it for the first time. They all looked above the door.

"Bar Foam. Argh! No wonder!" Yep, we'd officially been Ibiza-ed. We could go home happy now we'd been to a foam party. . .

Showers and a change of clothes later, we breezed through the doors of Manumission, VIP wristbands on. "Jeeeeeeez – it's huge!" Sam whistled as we were greeted by a giant aircraft hangar of a place. An ornately decorated stage worthy of a London theatre dominated the far end on the floor below. With grand pillars standing guard either side, cloaked in swathes of red velvet, glitterballs overhead and the Manumission logo hanging as a backdrop floor to ceiling, it was an impressive sight. A shabby-looking square swimming pool lit up the middle of the dance floor, the DJ booth suspended on a bridge above it. There was a long low-lit bar behind us, people flirting to get served first. We stood openmouthed on the upper level looking out over the whole club, except it wasn't the whole club, there were still so many more rooms to explore, an outside terrace and a space odyssey dome of a thing with a bar inside. The club was decked out in plush reds and gold. Flashing lights and more glitterballs and decorations hung from gantries across the whole ceiling, vying for space with what looked like trapeze wires!

"It's the biggest club in the world!" Gemma shouted above the music, which was quite hard, not really my cup of tea. "Sol said VIP was straight ahead, come on!" Gemma pied-pipered the way to our own little piece of exclusivity.

"Is this it?" Katie asked noticeably disappointed as we flashed our wristbands to the bouncer who must have got out of prison that day. "It's not as big as Pacha's."

"Don't ask me," I said. "Maybe there's another bit we can't see." Ropes separated us from the great unwashed, policed by bouncers with walkie-talkies. Round tables were dotted about – the area was narrow and already full of bodies, dancing, chatting, drinking, whatever. A balcony ran the whole length of it so only one side was exposed to the public.

"Can you see anyone famous?" Gemma asked.

"Not yet, give it time. P Diddy's supposed to be on the island this week – Sol said. Maybe we'll see him," Sam informed us.

"Bottles of Cristal!" Katie exclaimed at the table decorations. "Are we allowed to drink them?" I should coco.

Then I spotted him: Matt. He was chatting to Sol, so I could study his profile. Greek God, anyone? With his aquiline nose and strong jaw-line he really stood out amongst the mere mortals. Listen to me – I sound like a *Mills and Boon*! Elephants inconsiderately trampolined in my tummy – it was the first time I'd seen him since doing IT. Eeeeek! What if he didn't fancy me any more? What if he realized it was all a big mistake and I had the sexual prowess of an ironing board, would I be cool and not cry? I'd spent the last three days trying not to think about him (unsuccessfully) or talk about him, and concentrate instead on my DJing, 'cos tomorrow was my first proper night. But sometimes even playing had felt like a chore 'cos all I wanted to do was kiss him. I was turning into a sad loser. I was turning into Katie pre-dumping.

I glanced round and noticed Sam had gone white. "Are you OK?" I squeezed her hand.

"I think I need the loo." And she ran from VIP into the club – she looked like she was going to be sick.

chapter

I followed her through the crowd and caught up with her by a bar near the entrance.

"Hey – wait for me, that's not the loo."

She turned round, her eyes looking like a startled rabbit. "I'm going home, Lilla, I'm really sorry."

"But we just got here! Do you feel ill? I didn't think you'd had that much to drink."

"I haven't, it's not that. . ."

"Well, what then? You can't go, it's my birthday,

I want you here, and Sol's waiting for you in VIP." She flinched at the mention of his name. "Sam, what's going on?"

"I can't go in there, I can't do this, be his girlfriend, it's not me."

"You've been doing it pretty well up till now," I said. "Don't you like him any more?"

"I do, loads." She paused, looking like she was holding back tears. "What if it all goes Pete Tong and I get hurt?"

Sam was having a wobbly. "Come on, let's get a drink, we need a few shots."

After two tequila shots, she seemed a bit more like Sam again. "Before this holiday I'd told myself that boys just ruin things, get in the way of what you want to do. So I've always kept it casual, bailed out before it got messy." She sighed. "My mum always told me never to get married – get a career, make something of myself." Yes, we all knew about Sam's mum – bitter and twisted. But look at my mum, she's successful, yeah, she might hate my dad, but she has a career and me. What more could she want?! Ha ha. "But Sol's the first boy I've ever actually liked, as well as fancied. He wants to set up his own record label, he's going to help me with my holiday assignment if I get into journalism college – he encourages me and we talk about everything. To go from nothing to full-blown liking someone is just too freaky."

Wow, this was the most I'd ever heard Sam offload about herself. "But, Sam, that's great. Sounds like a proper relationship to me." Like I knew what I was talking about! One lost cherry later and suddenly I'm an expert. "He likes you, you like him, why can't you just see what happens?"

"I don't know, I'm crap, I guess. . ."

"You're not crap, you're great! One more for the road?" And I ordered another shot – we were going to be falling over at this rate. Just as we slammed the glasses down, Katie appeared through the throng.

"You two! We thought you'd copped off with someone else." As if. "You're missing all the fun – P Diddy's in VIP with an entourage the size of So Solid. Come on!" Time to face the music. I gripped Sam's hand and we soldiered after Katie. I was having an attack of nerves too. It will be fine, it will be fine – my chosen mantra for today.

And it was. "Happy Birthday, beautiful," Matt whispered into my ear after he'd kissed my lips hello – pants, say goodbye. He had the ability to transform my insides into warm honey. "Where'd you disappear to? One minute you were there, the next minute vanished. You OK? Not too drunk yet?"

"Not drunk enough!" As if by magic a glass of golden bubbles appeared in my hand – talk about service! Can it be my birthday every day, please? I checked out Sam and Sol and they looked really into each other – I guess it was cool with them too.

"We should go for a wander in a bit," Matt shouted in my ear. "There's so much more than this shitty little bit, but it's free, so that's why we're here! Look out for the people doing their laundry, and the potato peelers!" Apparently there was a laundrette where you could take off your clothes and wash and dry them. Something I find myself desperate to do on a night out!

"So where's P Diddy?" I asked Katie.

"At the back, next to the balcony." I craned my neck over someone's shoulder and could see a large crowd of what looked like minders: garbed in black, shades on, mean-looking; and inside them I glimpsed a gaggle of beautiful babes, blondes, black women, all in skimpy clothes. No P Diddy.

"He'll be sat down with two or three of the

221

girls, drinking Cristal, sending out scouts to find more girls — he's a right Romeo!" Matt knew all about it.

I really wanted to go and observe the rest of the club, but half of me wanted to see if P Diddy really was behind the blockade, dressed in some outrageously naff designer clobber.

"We're going for a wander — want to come?" Sam was holding Sol's hand. "Sol said the music's better downstairs." Katie was up for it too. Gemma was chatting up some young trendy boy who looked familiar, then I realized he was from some really crap hospital drama at home. She wasn't going anywhere until she'd cracked him, I could tell.

It wasn't so hot outside VIP; my bustier had started to stick to me. Matt held my hand as he guided me down the steps swamped by a sea of people all heading the same way. The Coco Loco lounge was really small compared to the cavernous main room, but the beats were better. We all managed to get halfway in, people tutting as we squirmed past. When the DJ played a really well-known tune, tingles careered down my spine and Matt and I jumped up and down, laughing like loons. The whole room was tuned into the same frequency, bodies synchronized, moving with the beats, happy, laughing, better than anything. Katie had a circle of admirers round her – she was showing off her new dance routine, not really noticing the stir she was causing in her black gypsy top and extremely low-slung, bum-hugging black flares.

"Have you seen who's on the decks?" Sam shouted above the music to me after another storming tune hit the floor running.

"Yeah – it's Steve Wheeler, isn't it?" Matt said 'cos he could see above all the heads. I could feel the colour drain from my cheeks. Argh!!!!!!

"What's *he* doing here?" I hissed. Dad didn't say he was playing Manumission tonight. In fact, I thought he only ever played at Nectar. He knew we were coming here and he'd said nothing! He was spying. . .

"He probably got asked at the last minute," Matt said. "He sometimes plays here when someone's ill or 'exhausted' – used to be him pulling that sort of trick!" he laughed.

"Do you want to try another room?" Sam asked, noticing my rapid deflation. I shook my head, I didn't know what to do. I can't explain why it bothered me that Dad was the DJ tonight. I wasn't prepared for it. Don't get me wrong, I had seen him DJ in the past, but at parties, not in a professional capacity where he was in control of *my* night. It didn't feel right.

"What's the matter?" Matt asked. "Do you feel OK?" I felt guilty 'cos he was so concerned and I was being a brat.

I needed to have a word with myself. . . "I'm just going to sit down a minute." I didn't even look back, just pushed my way to the door, headed up some stairs back the way we'd come and then out on to a terrace, bypassing the VIP area. I jumped when I felt a hand touch the middle of my back as I was deliberating where to sit. Matt was behind me.

"Hey – you were on a mission. I couldn't keep up."

We were under the stars and a welcoming breeze played round the edges of my top, finding its way in, cooling my skin. The terrace was quite busy, lots of clubbers slumped on seats, smoking and staring at the stars like they'd never seen them before. In one corner there were about fifteen people peeling potatoes into buckets, a sign above them telling them that when they'd finished they should leave the peelers for the next person who came along! I guessed this was the come-up zone, the place where you went if you were having a moment, when the rush was all a bit too much and you couldn't even speak. I felt like that now without the drugs, thank you very much!

"You can see your villa from here," Matt said, taking my hand and walking me over to the view. It was so dark all we could see were the murky outlines of the hills nestling in the shadows, and pinpricks of lights speckled here and there where villas made themselves known. Privilege sat between Jesus and San Antonio, meaning we could see Ibiza Old Town blazing in the distance, its heartbeat apparent even from this distance.

A woman was giving head massages and another henna tattoos. I don't think anyone here was in the right frame of mind for either. "Are you going to tell me what this is about?" he asked as we sat down. How could I explain? I felt a twat, it was hardly tantamount to abuse, was it? My dad is the DJ and it's ruining my night. Get a grip. . .

I took a deep breath and suddenly all the pent-up feelings about Dad, Lena, his shitty friend Dave, all came tumbling out. "Steve Wheeler's my dad, and I just feel weird about people knowing."

"Ahh," was all he said. I waded through the

wedding; how Mum would overreact when she read about the engagement and should I tell her first; how much I hated his best man; Lena's obsession with *OK Magazine*; how Dad was on the slide downhill with his DJing; how I didn't want him to know about my DJing 'cos he'd already made it clear he thought I'd be shit; my fear of anyone finding out he was my dad in case no one took me seriously and how on my birthday this was the last place I wanted to see him. It's good to talk!

"Well, that explains why you ran out the shop when he was in the other day. It's all becoming clear." He put his arm around me and hugged me. "You've got a lot going on inside your head, haven't you?" I nodded, for the first time realizing that *had* been in there all the time, waiting to spill out. It's amazing what goes on without you knowing, isn't it? "Lilla, I'm a bloke and by gene selection, not much good at this sort of thing." I laughed. "But what I can tell you is that you can't be worrying about your mum and how she feels about the wedding. She's a grown-up – she'll get over it. Be happy for your dad that he's got someone nice. I've met Lena a few times in the shop and she's a genuine person." I knew that – I did like her too, even though she was making me wear green in *OK*. "And your dad isn't on the skids, his nights at Nectar are pretty good. Just 'cos he's been out of the music limelight for a while doesn't mean anything. He's still a legend. Ignore what journalists say and those cheesy *OK* articles – the Slinky crew think he's a star. As for your paranoia, forget it, he'll be as proud as punch and think you're great – why wouldn't he? You're his kid, after all! I think you should tell him about Bar Lorca. He'll find out sooner or later."

I stared at him – that told me. I tried to agree with everything apart from the part about telling Dad about me DJing. I wasn't ready for that yet. "Now, are you going to come back and see your dad spin those famous wheelers of steel? You have to admit, he's on fire tonight."

"OK, as long as we can keep this a secret, that he's my dad. I want to play a few more nights before anyone else finds out. I don't know why, it would just make me feel better."

"You're the boss." And he pulled me to my feet. . .

chapter

twenty-three

The rest of Dad's set was excellent and I gave in, dancing with everyone, but we didn't go and say hello. There was a stage show starting upstairs, so we decided to check it out in the main arena. It was a mosh pit, bodies everywhere, all turned towards the stage. Matt nudged me and pointed above it — sequinned trapeze artists swung, throwing each other carelessly from one precarious wire to another. I held my breath, waiting for someone to fall — it really was spectacular. Acrobats in lurid Lycra costumes tumbled out of the wings and flipped back and forwards while half-naked fire-eaters juggled batons of flames, extinguishing them with their mouths. Erotic dancers covered in red and pink feathers and nipple tassels and not much else shimmied across the stage, simulating sex. All over the club, glittery girls and boys popped up on podiums, herding us into the centre like sheep.

We found ourselves at the edge of the pool; the smell of all the chemicals wafting off the water was quite foul. As we were watching the spectacle, one of the boys who'd been pestering Katie earlier sidled up behind her, pinching her bum. "Oi!" She turned round and he smiled. He looked absolutely wasted, eyes on stalks, God knows what he was on. "Don't do that!"

"What?" He held his hands up in an innocent man gesture. She let it go and he did it again once her back was turned.

"You minger. Leave me alone, PLEASE!"

"Come on, you were flirting with me down there, don't say you don't like me."

"I don't even remember you."

"You OK, Katie?" I asked, noticing his irritating slack-jawed grin.

"Yes, he was just going, weren't you?"

"No. I'm watching the show." She moved nearer the pool to get away, but he followed. Matt was about to have a go when Katie flipped.

"Just fuck off!" she cried. "I'm not interested."

"Not until you have a drink with me." And he tried to step closer, but Katie had had enough, people were watching her now instead of the show. She sidestepped out of the way so he filled the place she had been standing.

"Maybe this is what you're after!" And she sprang at him like a whirling dervish, propelling him into the pool backwards, catching him off guard. His face was a picture – total shock as he hit the water, arms windmilling frantically. "Drink that!"

"Go, Katie!" Sam shouted.

"Come on, Mohammed Ali, security will throw you out, let's go!" Matt grabbed her and the crowd parted, people wanting to give Katie a high five, clapping her on the back as we hurried past. I looked behind, no one was helping him out of the pool – he was still flapping around shouting. It's a pity you can't catch crabs from green algae. . .

Safely inside VIP, we breathed a sigh of relief. "I cannot believe you pushed him in!" Sol laughed. "I wish I'd had a camera."

"He deserved it. No more Mrs Nice Guy," and she growled in an unconvincing manner. I guessed the nasty texts from Tom had fuelled her temper.

"Girls, guess what? We've been invited to a party at P Diddy's villa." Gemma was beside herself as we approached her.

"How? What've you been doing?"

Apparently Gemma had been spotted by one of the minders and asked over for a drink and duly abandoned Actor Boy for more exciting things and a flasher crowd.

"So, did you actually meet him?" Katie gasped.

"Not really. There were too many people, but I got a good look – he looks a lot older than in the magazines and he was wearing a really naff white suit, not my type." As if Puffy would even give a toss what Gemma thought! "One of his minders, Jerome, said I could come back with him to the villa, everyone's going, apparently Geri Halliwell is supposed to be there later." She waved to this guy Jerome and he smiled back – a brick shithouse of a guy with railway-sleeper shoulders. I wouldn't want to mess.

"But how come we're all invited as well?" I asked, smelling a rat.

"Err . . . I just said you were Steve Wheeler's

daughter and could you and our mates come too – he said why not." She pulled an "I hope you don't mind" face.

"*You're* Steve Wheeler's daughter?" Sol was amazed. "No wonder you're so into DJing." Oh no! "We love your dad at Slinky, he's hysterical. I remember this one time when he did this marathon set at Space, had done so much coke he wet himself 'cos he wouldn't leave the decks to go for a wee – got paranoid someone else would take his place. What a legend!" What a nightmare more like. I *knew* this would happen. . .

"Sol!! I don't think Lilla wants to hear what a caner her dad used to be. A bit of respect, please!" Sam had a go. He apologized, I think the horror on my face said it all.

"So are we going to P Diddy's party or what?" Gemma asked, getting anxious, her needs at the top of the list as usual. "They're leaving at four." It was quarter to. Where had the time gone?

"P Diddy? A party – what do you think?" Katie cried, hyper from her heroics by the pool.

We clambered into a people-carrier paid for by Jerome. It was still dark outside Manumission, and the drive took about twenty minutes up winding tracks, the headlights picking out olive trees and the occasional villa. My memory goes a bit hazy here 'cos when we arrived, it was rammed and there was a woman dressed as a devil handing out champagne in flutes you could have used as bird baths. I remember marble pillars, crystal chandeliers, mahogany just about everywhere and floor to ceiling windows framing a view worthy of a movie's opening credits. Glamorous people were flitting here and there, all older than us, and some of them looked familiar from *OK Magazine* and those crappy Sunday supplements. Z list celebs probably. . .

Next thing I knew, we were all in a Jacuzzi in our underwear overlooking the hills as the sun came up: me, Matt, Sam, Sol and Katie. Gemma was AWOL. We had managed to nab a couple of bottles of champagne from one of the tables – Matt expertly blew the first cork into the back of someone's head. He wasn't amused!

"Do you think we should look for Gemma?" Katie asked. "She's been gone for about half an hour."

"In a bit," Sam said. "I'm sick of being her mum, she'll be fine. She's probably telling P Diddy that he should think about changing his style, or something."

Talking of P Diddy, he certainly wasn't around. Come to think of it, there weren't any real celebs to speak of and definitely no Geri Halliwell. . .

The bubbles had gone to my head 'cos I felt brave enough to lean over and kiss Matt on the mouth – he was looking so lush, his tanned chest poking out of the froth. I wanted to get him home and hnnnggggg—

"Hey! You guys, can I come in?" Gemma tottered down the garden holding two flutes of champagne and kept stopping to swig out of one of them. She looked a mess – even Sam looked shocked and she's seen her in a state a few times, but this took the biscuit. Her mascara was running down her face, lipstick was smeared on her top and had bled round her mouth and her trousers had three fag burns in them on the knees. One of her gold hoop earrings was missing and her hair looked like it had been superglued in a hurricane. The other party guests were looking at her like she was a freak show and cleared a path for her so they didn't get in the way.

"What the fuck happened to you?" Sam shouted as she got nearer. I could see a twig sticking out of her mop.

"Oh, I fell in a bush back there." Jeeeeez. We

couldn't take her anywhere. She sat down next to the Jacuzzi. She kept licking her lips and her eyes were all over the shop, really mad-looking. "I'm coming in," and she just got in in her clothes, stilettos too! "It's a bit hot!"

"Gemma, are you OK? You've gone white," Sol asked.

"I'm fine. Look, I got you some cocktails, Jerome made them in the kitchen – here, try it."

I took it but Matt stopped me drinking it. "What's it called, Gemma?" he asked.

"Err . . . Champagne Supernova, I think." She really did look white now.

"Christ – how many have you had?" Sol asked as Matt tipped it on to the grass, taking the other one away from her lips and doing the same.

She went quiet and thought. "I can't remember. . . Four or five?"

Sol shook his head. "You know what's in them, don't you?" he asked.

She was silent. "Gemma! What did he put in them?" Sam asked getting wound up.

"I don't know, I didn't see. I know it was something in a bag."

"Coke, he was putting coke in there," Matt said. "Champagne Supernovas are coke and champagne."

"Eugh!" Katie grimaced. "Why waste good champagne with fat Coke. It must taste foul."

"No, cocaine," Matt said. Katie looked shocked, we all were.

"You took cocaine?" Sam asked in a strangled voice. "And you offered it to Lilla?"

"I didn't know!" But somehow, none of us believed her. She must have known – she saw him do it! "I'm going to be sick."

Matt got up and dragged her out of the Jacuzzi just before she puked everywhere. And that was it, the end of the night – she didn't stop being sick and went into a sort of faint. Sam started to panic.

A tide of anxiety was crashing in my tummy too. How were we going to get home? We couldn't get a taxi, they were all busy ferrying clubbers.

"Call Lena!" Sam ordered. "She'll come and get us." Normally, I would have told her to get lost, but right now it was the only sane option and with Gemma being sick every five minutes, what else could I do?

"Philippa! What are you calling me at this time for?" Lena asked. Nectar would have closed about an hour ago and she was doing the takings.

I blurted out what had happened, Champagne Supernovas and all, and told her where we were –

Sol knew. "I'll be there in ten minutes, you're not that far from us." She sounded really pissed off. I was gonna get a bollocking for this, I just knew it.

We sat outside the gates looking like refugees, Gemma propped up against them, plastic bag handy for the car journey. She was whiter than ever and green in places. "I'm sorry," was all she could whisper.

The car pulled up and Lena got out, a worried look on her face. I was going to KILL Gemma for this. . .

chapter
twenty-four

"Has she woken up yet?" I asked Sam when I surfaced at about two, leaving Matt in bed.

"No." She was reading a magazine under an umbrella, pint of water by her side. "I'll tell you one thing, Lilla, this is the last time. She was on a collision course last night, she doesn't think about anyone but herself." Sam was fuming.

It had been a nightmare. Lena had brought us back to the gnome villa and helped us undress Gemma. She sorted her out with special rehydration sachets to get fluids back in her and stayed until she went to sleep at about eight this morning. But she didn't bollock me at all, surprisingly. "Make her drink orange juice when she wakes up, and only let her eat small amounts." I forgot she was an expert at sorting out people on a coke comedown. . .

"Lena, you won't tell Dad, will you?" I asked nervously, silently pledging to gladly wear any shade of green she threw at me for the wedding.

"Philippa, who d'you think I am?" she said. "As if I'd do that. This is between us. I'm just glad you're so sensible and stayed well clear. You of all people know how evil that stuff is." I did, and that's why I was smarting so much from Gemma being such a dick. She knew how much I hated the idea of drugs and yet she took them right in front of me, on my birthday too! "Anyway, he'd go mad!" she said. "And you know what that's like. . ."

When Gemma did surface, we were all eating lunch under the vines. Sol had gone to work, but Matt had taken the day off and made us all bacon sarnies. She wandered outside, wrapped in a sarong, looking like she needed an emergency face iron, the last traces of make-up still clinging to her eyelids. "Is there a sandwich for me too?" she had the cheek to ask. No one said anything. Matt got up to make her one, but I pulled him down; she would have to do some serious grovelling before we made her food.

She sat down at the edge of the table in silence. "Look, I'm really sorry about getting so pissed last night and being sick. I feel like death if that makes up for it."

"Good, I'm glad you feel like shit," Sam snarled. "We're not feeling too hot either."

"I don't think anything can make up for you last night," I said quietly, suddenly not wanting my sandwich. "You were out of order, Gem."

"I was drunk. God, I'm sorry. We've all been there. . ."

"Can't you remember *anything* from the party?" Katie asked, puzzled at Gemma's blasé attitude.

"I remember drinking champagne then being sick and getting a cab back, but that's about all. Nothing too dramatic." She looked wary.

"You stupid cow!" Sam shouted. "You haven't got a fucking clue, have you?"

Gemma jumped, the recently returned colour fading from her cheeks. "What? What did I do?"

We all looked at each other and I nodded. So I

told her everything; her face was stony all the way through.

"Gemma, this is the last time," Sam said angrily. "No more car crashes, no more expecting people to run around looking after you, it's got to stop."

"Or you'll do what?" she said defiantly, but with a wobble in her voice.

"I'm not doing anything any more, that's the point. You're on your own. You get in trouble, you get yourself out of it." She gave Gemma a Look.

"You put me in a very difficult position last night with Lena," I said, worn out. She looked at the floor. "You *knew* Jerome was putting something in those drinks, even if you didn't know what it was. You know how much I hate drugs, how they fucked up my dad. How could you?"

It was all too much — she burst into tears. "I don't remember! Not any of that. . ." She put her head in her hands and sobbed. Katie got up and sat next to her to give her a hug. "I'm sorry, I'm sooooo sorry. I hate myself. I promise I won't do it again."

Sam snorted in disbelief. "I mean it!" Gemma cried looking up. "It scares me, the fact that I can't remember. Anything could have happened."

"It did," Katie said softly. "You have to slow

down, not be such a whirlwind. You can have fun without the extreme, you know. We all manage it!"

"I know, but I find it hard." She shrugged helplessly. "I feel more . . . alive if I have a drink – or ten," she laughed sarcastically. "I guess I knew Sam would always make sure I was OK. . ."

"But, Gemma, we all go to college this year, what were you going to do then? Find some other mug to look after you?" Sam said.

A tear slid down Gemma's cheek. "No, I'll never find anyone as good as you, Sam, you're my best friend and I'm sorry I've been such a tool."

Sam suddenly stopped being angry and leaned over and kissed her head. "You idiot," she said affectionately.

"Right, Gemma, do you want that bacon sandwich now?" Matt said, jumping up, embarrassed at having to witness all this raw girlie emotion.

She nodded. "Thanks, Matt."

I was late for work. Matt was taking me in on the moped. I'd had to go back to bed. "I can't go – I feel so shit," I'd moaned at him from underneath the sheets.

"Lilla, I have to go in with hangovers. You've had

all day to recover. Come on – get out of bed!"
Where's my sympathy?

My record bag was digging into my throat, but I couldn't move it or I'd fall off the back. This was my first full night at Bar Lorca, nine till midnight. I was absolutely bricking it, but Matt (surrounded by stars and a halo) was going to stay all night, and Sol and Sam said they'd meet us there later. Katie and Gemma stayed in watching satellite movies, I think Gemma needed a night in!

I'd run in the door, straight to the decks, Charlie wasn't around, thank God. Kelly was there and she waved as I dashed past, nearly breaking my ankle in Gemma's "glam" stiletto heels and tight jeans. Matt went home to have a shower and change and then said he'd be back. I jumped on the decks and kicked off. There were quite a few punters in drinking beers at the bar. More than last time; I had no time to worry about anything other than doing a good job. I had the shock of my life when I looked up after the second record, two DJ friends of Dad's were sat at the back by the loos sipping beers: Dan Frank and Ben Le Quesne, quite big names in my book! They were really good; I'd seen them play at Milo a few times. They didn't know who I was though, phew. I'd only met them twice and I *had* been fifteen.

"Lilla!" It was Charlie. I was going to get bollocked for being late. "Well done, you look great. The punters like a girl to look sexy." And he winked, yuk. "See, I'm right, those two guys over there, they're big-name DJs, they've sent you over a drink." And he plonked a beer down next to the mixer. After last night, I was wary of drinking anything that I hadn't seen opened myself.

"Thanks." I looked over and they raised their bottles to me and smiled. I nervously smiled back and carried on choosing the next tune. I let the music take over and was pulling out all sorts of sleeves from my box, oblivious to specific people, just being aware of the vibe of the room and what it needed. Matt turned up and sat at the bar with a beer, he got me one and I drank it gratefully (hair of the dog), leaving the other one untouched. Sam and Sol rocked up soon after. By eleven it was heaving and a raucous crowd were shouting their orders at the bar. Charlie kept coming and telling me I was sexy. I ignored him and smiled sweetly while mentally crunching his balls.

I was bent over my record box, rifling through, when a familiar gravelly voice made me jump. "D'you have any Rod Stewart?"

"Dad!" I didn't know what to do. Tumbleweed

whooshed past the decks, followed by a water trough and cowboy hat. It was the Wild Wild West: Wheeler and Daughter faced each other across the decks. "What are you doing here?"

"Oh, you know, having a drink." He smirked, the old Wheeler devil still in him.

"You've given up."

He raised a glass full of what looked like water. "Better hurry and choose the next one or you'll run out of time." Then he sauntered back to the bar where I saw Lena chatting with Sam, Matt and Sol. They must have told him! Bastards. I *was* running out of time and suddenly couldn't make a decision about what to play next. Whatever I chose would have to be amazing 'cos now it mattered more than before. The other record was still immersed in the meat of the tune, but any minute now it was going to start stripping down. I made a choice and stuck with it, bringing it in, playing with the EQs, jazzing it up, nothing too fancy, just enough to say, "Look, I can do this, it's not a fluke." Ha, put that in your Rizla and smoke it!

Dad wasn't even paying attention, Lena looked over and waved, pulling an "I am not worthy face" at me. I laughed. Dad had gone to chat to Ben and Dan and they were all laughing, probably at me.

Sod them! Enough people thought I was good, I thought I was good, I didn't need approval . . . did I? I got my head down, selecting booty-shaking tunes that had people nodding heads at the bar. I got a few guys (not bad-looking!) hanging round, trying to get my attention, buying me drinks, they gave up after I ignored them, giving my love instead to my slices of vinyl. "Hey, Lilla, did you know Steve Wheeler's in tonight?" Charlie shouted in my ear as I came to the end of my set. He was collecting my empties, so the place was clear for the next DJ I'd yet to meet. "He hasn't been in here for years, not since he fell off the wagon." It seemed the whole world and his dog knew about my dad's private life. His own fault. . .

"Yes, he's come to see me." Charlie laughed in a "You should be so lucky" kind of way. I slipped my headphones off. "He's my dad." I didn't feel weird saying it, it felt OK. And the satisfaction of seeing his face fall was enough to outweigh any misgivings I had. I could tell he believed me – why lie about something like that? He was probably shitting himself in relief about the dirty deals he hadn't yet pulled to a) rip me off, or b) try it on. Ha ha. I hadn't realized up until then that Dad could be a deterrent as well. He mumbled something like "No wonder," whatever that meant, and made a sharp exit to take cover behind the bar.

I looked over at Dad when I came off the decks. He was sat down with Ben and Dan – his face obscured, the others were milling about him, chatting. Matt came over to carry my bag – my DJ bitch! I must have looked worried or something. "I didn't know he was coming, honest!" I raised an eyebrow. "OK, Sol told Lena this morning while you were in the loo, asked her if she and Steve were going to watch your professional debut. You never told him not to say anything." This bit was true. "I didn't want to get involved with family stuff, Lilla. I'd just been rescued by your future step-mum after taking you to a party where one of your friends took so much coke she passed out. I didn't feel like I had any right to start issuing orders about what they couldn't do." I knew he was right, but I still felt kind of miffed. "Mmmmm," was about all I could manage. He knew how much this bothered me. "I mean, who am I to talk? It's not like we're a long-term item that your dad even knows about. We just met!"

Now I felt sick – what did that mean? That we were just a holiday fling, that he didn't see it going anywhere? I obviously *was* shit in bed. I could feel my eyes start stinging – for CHRIST'S sake, Lilla, what happened to the "I don't care if he never rings" 'tude? Packed its bags and emigrated, that's what! A drip on the end of my nose threatened to slide into my lipgloss, I wiped it as we pushed through the wall of people to get to Dad's table. Smoke hung in a thick fog about a centimetre above our heads; I was suffocating.

"Philippa! You were magnificent!" Lena gave me a big hug. "We had no idea you were *this* good. . ." She passed me a drink, a champagne cocktail of some sort.

"Lilla, I'm so sorry," Sol whispered in my ear as Lena tapped Dad on the shoulder. "I didn't know it was a secret – I feel really bad. If it's any consolation, you were blinding." I gave him a watery smile; I didn't trust myself to speak. Why was I being such a weirdo? Dad looked up, Dan and Ben started cheering and clapping when they saw me. Punters were craning their necks to ogle at Dad and see what all the fuss was about.

Dad pushed his chair back and stood up, his face a slab of granite. Now I knew what people meant when they said a room stood still. Everyone else just melted away. I felt like we were sizing each other up before a fight. But then something extraordinary happened: his jaw cracked and a smile spread like melted butter across his face. He stepped forward and took me in his arms, squeezing me so tight my ribs cracked. "My little girl," he said in my ear. "You were fucking brilliant." That did it, the tears that had lurked minutes before spilled out and I was powerless to stop them. Cue embarrassing parental bonding moment – thank God *OK Magazine* weren't on hand to take it all down for posterity!

chapter

twenty-five

If this really were a movie and not life, we would be careering towards the title sequence now, loose ends being tied up left right and centre before the grand finale, everyone heading off into the sunset with a big fat paycheque. Not quite so neat here, pop pickers. After a two-week emotional rollercoaster (four girls, two boys, one villa, two mopeds, one restaurant runner, one mad dad, one lost cherry, a million gnomes, Champagne Supernovas – I could go on), we headed into the second two weeks ready for a rest from any more turmoil. Like that was gonna happen! But it would take another book to explain, so here goes the nutshell version.

Four days after my homecoming at Bar Lorca, we rang the UK for our A Level results. Katie got four As, med school a dead cert. She was rather quiet for someone who'd achieved her ultimate goal. But she soon snapped out of it when she got a phone call from home. "You'll never guess what? Tom fucked up all his retakes – he's not got into med school. I'm freeeeeee!" She'd been dreading going in September, knowing he would be there like a bad smell. Not any more. . .

Sam got an A, B and C – whooping and drunkenness follow tout suite. Me – two Ds and a C (I cannot even believe I did that well, I did so little work). I could go to Uni – notice the lack of cheerleaders and fireworks accompanying that discovery. Now I had to face it – the rest of my life. . . Roll out the Persian rug and a big broom. Meanwhile – Gemma, oh dear, one C and two fat Fs. Arse. She took it rather well, joking that at least she could go back to school where there would be a whole new fresh supply of boys she could take out on the town and corrupt. Sam raised an eyebrow, only to be met with, "For Christ's sake, I was joking. I'm turning over a new leaf!" I believed her though. She needed to sort a few things out, and getting into Uni was something she really did want to do, so clubbing, getting pissed and wasting whole weeks at a time were things that would have to sit on the reserve bench. She could do all that at Uni, but she had to get in first!

Money was now tighter than a duck's arse — even after contributions from my earnings, drinking before we went out and Lena pulling every string possible so all clubs were free — we were still broke. There were a few more big nights at Pacha and one Sunday afternoon and evening at Space where Fatboy Slim played — it was awesome. Clubbing in daylight was a new experience and the amount of people that hadn't gone to bed from the night before was ridiculous. However the big surprise was Nectar — it was a revelation. Dad was phenomenal; he really worked the crowd, connecting with us all, tuning in to what we wanted to hear. The club itself was small with lights set into the floor to guide you to the bars and loos. There was a stream running through the centre, lit up with spots, and a comfy room with lush brown leather banquettes that offered privacy. It all added up to an intimate feel, rather than the needle in a haystack experience of the larger venues. The crowd was very mixed, quite a few older people, the ones who remembered Dad in his heyday and came to relive their misspent yoof. Not an England shirt in sight!

"Honestly, Lils, this is going to be next year's big pull, forget all the super-clubs, people want to get back to basics, good music and the personal touch, not aircraft hangars with no soul." Sam loved it – I couldn't agree more.

Gemma did surprise us all and calm down quite a bit. She was still Gemma, so the poor boys never got a holiday from her constant sharking, though I never noticed Dan/Pete/Tim/Jake/Mark/whoever complain. We'd say hello in the morning and then never see them again.

"I quite like this no hangover thing I've got going," she said one morning, rather smugly I thought, 'cos I was feeling rather rough. We didn't expect her to give up drinking, but we now went out without having to worry who was looking out for her. Some nights she put me to shame by sticking to a few drinks and then water. "It's a new experience, Lilla. I like being in control for a change. Means I'm less likely to pull with beer goggles on!" She had a point; all her flings had been very cute. We'll see . . . one day at a time as they say in, er . . . AA!

Sam and Sol saw a lot of each other as the holiday drew to a close. She had to write a piece for her course (natch she got in with her grades!), and she chose to write about the difficulties of breaking into the music biz when you're not working in the commercial sector (i.e. all the crap like *Pop Idol* and boy bands, etc). Sol introduced her to people that came in the shop and she nervously interviewed them. He took her to see underground DJs and she loved every second. Sometimes Matt and I went too – it was useful for me to see what other people were playing.

In the final week, we had a repeat performance of the wobbly in Manumission. I walked in on her in the bathroom one morning after he'd left for work. She looked like she'd been crying and was furiously splashing her face with cold water. "Sam!" She tried to pretend nothing was wrong and I left it at that, but that afternoon Katie, Sam and I went for a hike in the hills to catch the view from behind the villa. Out of breath and red from the effort we flopped on the powdery earth at the top of the highest point. The whole island lay at our feet, undulating like the waves that crashed on its shores. From up here all we could hear were crickets, the occasional tractor, birds calling to each other in the trees and our hearts pounding in our ears. I lay back and plucked a strand of leathery grass from the spikes prodding the back of my head and set about chewing it while contemplating the vast expanse of sky overhead.

"I can't believe we only have five days left," Katie said, sitting cross-legged with her back against a tree stump. "This has been the best holiday of my life." I looked at her, the sun highlighting the honey-blonde hair tucked behind her ears, and felt warm and fuzzy. She could have stayed in London, worked in Selfridges and been back with Tom – instead here she was, a different person, footloose and fancy-free, happy and having the best time! She'd been spending a lot of time with Andy at the beach on his days off and had gone out to the gay club with him and some dancers from Pacha in the town a few nights while we were on dates. She said she'd never had so much fun in her life before. "I've never had my bum pinched so much either. Gay men are just as bad," she'd laughed. There'd been a few snogs on nights out, but she was enjoying being single with no one to answer to, Tom's nasty stench a distant memory.

"Are you seeing Sol tonight?" Katie asked Sam innocently. No answer. "Sam?" We looked at her and just as we did, a tear slid down her face from under her sunnies. "Oh shit – what's the matter?" Katie cried. "You are still seeing him, aren't you?" She nodded, her nose gradually turning red with the effort of holding in tears. "So what's happened?"

"Nothing," she croaked. "Oh, everything. He told me he loved me last night."

"But that's wonderful!" Katie jumped up and crashed down next to her, I sat up and spat out the grass.

"No it isn't," she cried.

"Oh no, you don't feel the same way?" Katie questioned.

"That's the thing, I do, so much." She was wringing her hands.

"So what's the problem?"

"The ocean, the plane ride, London, home, that's the problem. He's going to be here for the rest of the summer and I'm going to be in London."

"But you'll see him when he comes home," I said.

"I won't. He's going to live in Manchester with two mates and start up his own record label. He's leaving Slinky." Oh. Fuckitydoodah.

"It's so typical, I finally meet a boy who rocks my world and he's going to live at the other end of the country."

"Sam, Manchester is hardly Australia," I said.

"You know what I mean."

"What does he think will happen?" Katie probed.

"He seems to think we'll see each other at weekends and he'll be down in town spotting talent and stuff, but it's just . . . oh, I don't know." She took off her glasses and squinted into the sun, rubbing her eyes. "I'm going to be so busy with my course and he's kidding himself if he thinks he'll have time to see me with his new record label launch. I hate not knowing what will happen."

"Well, you can only wait and see," Katie said sensibly. What else could we say?

"But I HATE that!" Sam cried like a spoiled child. "It messes with my head. Why can't I know now?"

"'Cos you can't," I shrugged helplessly. "That's life, innit?"

"Argh!" We understood her frustration 'cos it was sooo annoying, and for control freak Sam, this was a difficult one. "I just want to stop feeling like a lovesick puppy!"

"No you don't!" I laughed. "You love it, you do!" And deep down, she knew she did too.

chapter

"You look gorgeous in that colour!" Lena cooed as the shop assistant fussed with the zip. I turned and looked in a full-length mirror, admiring my reflection. Wow! I never thought it would suit me, but this pale sea-green silk set off my tan perfectly, not a corpse in sight. The dress was elegant (like me, yeah, right): a strapless bustier across my chest with a full-length straight skirt and massive side split. I'd need heels to stop me looking like a dwarf, though. "You'll be carrying a posy of purple orchids as well. Wait till your dad sees you." She'd gone all misty-eyed! I wasn't allowed to see what she was going to be wearing – it was a surprise.

Afterwards, she took me out to lunch at Lenny's Caff in Dalt Villa – an über-cool uncool place, if you know what I mean. It was hiding halfway up the hill overlooking the Old Town, down a cobbled side street next to a shop selling Moroccan-looking lampshades. It was a greasy spoon Ibiza-style, meaning you could get wine instead of a cuppa to ease the lard down your gullet. There were lots of Spanish people in there having tapas and reading the paper. Lena nodded to a few and air-kissed the guy I presumed was Lenny – in the middle-age departure lounge, brown-paper-bag skin, a hint of East End gangster about him. His caff was all wooden tables and chairs, red gingham tablecloths and walls plastered with pics of faces behind glass frames – all the people who had visited over the years and kept coming back. He shook my hand. "This must be Philippa. Pleased to meet you, darlin', heard a lot about you." I smiled, wondering what on earth had been said. "The usual, Leen?" he asked when we'd sat down, not bothering with menus.

With only a few days left, the girls were all out

making the most of it while I sat here waiting for lunch: Katie and Gemma with Andy at Salinas beach, and Sol had taken Sam out on a day trip to Formentera. No one wanted to think about going home, least of all me 'cos I was staying. On my own. I hadn't thought about my job at Bar Lorca, I never expected it to take off, but after my night there when Dad came to see me, it had got better and better. I think Charlie had told everyone I was Steve Wheeler's daughter, 'cos it was always packed and I got given the glory slot after my second week – midnight till three am, Fridays and Saturdays now.

Dad had told me after my gig that he'd never doubted I could DJ, he was more concerned I would turn out to be a chip off the old block and turn into a loony drug-crazed nutter, 'cos gear is virtually offered on a plate if you're a DJ. He could now see that that would never happen and I did explain he was a good advert for "Just saying no!" At least he laughed! He also offered me the spare room for the rest of the season. I really didn't want to go home, but I didn't want to stay with him either (ungrateful cow that I am) 'cos it would mean no privacy, but I had no choice. If I was going to work, I had to stay there, end of story. And

Matt (hubba hubba) was around till the end of September and I could always hang out with him – he'd made it perfectly clear I was very welcome! Jules's place was out of bounds – he was back soon to convalesce and no doubt regain his party spirit. I just knew I was going to miss the girls. We'd had such a great time and it wouldn't be the same without them.

Telling Mum had been hideous – not only had she seen *OK* by this point and knew about the wedding, but when I told her I was staying, DJing and living with Dad till I started Uni in September, I could hear the atom split from here. I can't even be bothered to go on about it. She just shouted: how could I deceive her all these years? Had Dad known, we were laughing at her behind her back – all the usual paranoia. When we spoke a few days later, she'd calmed down, and felt a bit stupid. I managed to make her believe Dad had no idea, that he was thrilled, really supportive and that seemed to snap her out of the bad cop rôle. I think maybe she missed me a bit. She even asked me what I would be wearing as a bridesmaid and laughed hysterically when I said green! Cheers, Mum.

"Penny for them?" Lena interrupted.

"Oh, nothing, I was just thinking how much I'm going to miss everyone when they go home."

"You'll meet lots of new people – that girl at the bar, Kelly? – she's nice." Yes, she was, and she'd invited me out a few times after work, but I always wanted to hang with my gang, get in some quality time before they disappeared. "And you've got Matt and Sol at Slinky."

"I know, it'll be great." But Lena wasn't stupid.

"I promise your dad and I won't get in the way – I've given him orders." I smiled, that wasn't going to be easy with Dad, who had suddenly taken a keen interest in my life now I had a job, and wanted to talk shop at every given opportunity. Not what I was expecting at all. "Talk of the devil. . ."

In he strolled, looking like he'd been groomed – new haircut and clean-shaven. Lenny fussed around, and Dad lapped it up, as usual. "Hi, girls," he growled in an ironic swaggering way. "Find any pretty dresses?" Lena told him about my outfit and he seemed pleased. "And any other news, major decisions?" he asked pointedly.

"No, you know I was waiting till you got here," Lena said. I had no idea Dad was joining us. Oh no, I had this sick feeling in my tummy – they were going to tell me something even bigger than getting married. I was going to have a little brother or sister. I just *knew* it! That's why there was the big rush on the wedding, why they wouldn't let us all stay with them, why Dad was all clucky about me all of a sudden, why—

"Philippa – you're in a dream world today," Lena said, laughing. "I just said, your dad and I have a proposal for you." Oh, here we go, babysitting duties. . .

"It was actually Sol who suggested it," Dad said.

"Yes, but I did think it as well," she replied testily. What was going on?

Before I could find out, Lenny came over with the food – enough to feed about twenty people. Lena's usual consisted of every tapas dish going and a Frisbee-sized tortilla cut into thick yellow wedges, warm egg oozing on to the plate. We started digging in, but my tummy was all scrunched up, waiting to hear whatever it was. "So, you were saying?" I prompted them.

Lena chewed her garlic prawn in an exaggerated manner, letting me know she had to finish eating before she could speak. "Yes. Your dad and I were seriously impressed with your DJing the other week, and I hear that Charlie is too – offering you the top billing."

"Yeerrrrsssss." Was this a school report: nice tunes, could do better with mixer technique?

"And now we know you're staying for the rest of the season for sure, we thought you might like to play at Nectar too."

Whoa! Stop the bus! "When?" I was in shock.

"Welllll, as soon as you like, really," Dad said helping himself to more paella. "Lena's idea was to have you and me on together one night a week, possibly a Saturday."

"You want *me* to be your warm-up woman?"

"Not as such, no, more of a partner in crime: Wheeler and Daughter, or something like that. Have a DJ duel each Saturday, one record on, one off, have a bit of a laugh."

"But I only just got the job at Bar Lorca. What will Charlie say?"

"That he discovered you, probably," Dad snorted. "Don't worry about him, I can have a word."

"No! No, this is all too soon." I was starting to panic. This was the reason why I hadn't wanted anyone to know who my dad was in the first place. "People will just think I got the job 'cos of you, 'cos you felt sorry for me, keep it in the family, you know, not take me seriously. . ."

"Philippa! Give me some credit!" Lena cried. "First and foremost, I am a businesswoman. I wouldn't even book a DJ if I thought they were crap and couldn't draw in the crowds. I've seen you play a few times." This was news to me. "And I've seen what you can do. You're the same age as a lot of the punters, you know what they want to hear and you listen to them. You've got a real talent, just like Steve."

Dad agreed. "Come on, Philippa, now's not the time to think of pride. Who cares how you got the break – you got Bar Lorca all on your own – you're excellent and far too good for that place." Hmmmm, maybe . . . this was proper stuff. "Believe me, you could wait for ever in there and never make it to a big club, no matter how good you are, this way you get there a bit sooner and have fun on the way with your old man." Putting it that way it sounded far more attractive. . . I guess he was right.

"Lenny – a bottle of your finest champoo, my old mucker!" Lena gave him a Look. "And an orange juice for me." That was it then, I was going to work with Dad – OMIGOD!

"Oh, yes, Steve," Lena said, "I've decided to move my office into the spare room for now so

Philippa can have the flat. That's if you don't mind it all being a bit cramped for a while — she'll need her own space." She smiled at me and Dad nodded in agreement.

Suddenly staying with rentals didn't seem too bad at all. . . Result!

I met Matt for coffee after work to tell him my news. We had got into a habit of doing that a few times a week when we weren't seeing each other in the evening. My paranoia about our relationship, whatever you want to call it, was unfounded. We were more than a holiday fling, I realized that when he started talking about when we got home, what we'd be doing, etc. All the others were going to Uni (apart from Gemma), but I felt I was only chasing it 'cos it was expected I would go, never mind if I wanted to or not. It was time to stop sweeping it under the carpet and face it — DJing was what I wanted to do and if I couldn't do that straight away, I needed a job to fund it. I was offered work at the Slinky shop in London because Sol was leaving — I gratefully took it in lieu of things not working out. But things move quickly in clubland, who knows, I could land something on the back of Ibiza. I wasn't going to count on it, though. Just making the decision alone felt like a great weight had been lifted off my chest.

"Just think, Lilla," Matt said, "this time next year you could be headlining at Space. Sol and I'll have to *pay* to see you!" Yeah, and I'll be living with you in a rock-star villa, loved up and cosy. Well, a girl can dream, can't she?

departures

Our last night in the villa was a drunken affair –
you're not shocked, are you? I think I was more
gutted than they were, being left on my own. After
packing our stuff we spent the evening drinking
the remains of the alcohol, inventing new
cocktails. The Kitchen Knife – tomato juice, rum
and lemonade (yuk), and the Wasted Clubber – fat
Coke, crème de cassis and vodka (not too bad)
were two of the most memorable ones. While
Katie and Sam manned the barbecue I showed

Gemma how to cue tunes on the decks for our disco – I was having a night off.

At around five am the cupboard had been stripped bare of any remaining alcohol (including the vile-tasting blue curaçao) and we'd all had a cry at least once, declared undying love for each other and vowed to have a reunion the minute we were all in the same country. We simultaneously passed out outside on sunbeds while far above us, the Ibizan dawn cracked the stars' hold on the sky, shooing them away. Another sun-blessed day beckoned, and we were missing it, snoring in the garden among our height-challenged housemates, the gnomes.

Lena dropped us at the Departures entrance. "I'll wait for you in the car park, Philippa." Sam, Gemma and Katie hugged her goodbye while I grabbed a trolley.

Wednesday afternoon, four weeks since our crash-landing in Ibiza. Another flight had come in and there were coaches everywhere, reps shouting, hassled-looking families, mums screeching at their kids to follow them and not wander off. I noticed some girls who looked the same age as us, wandering around looking lost, then spotting the taxi rank. I wondered if they would have an amazing time like we did.

We were desperately reliving our best moments, pushing the trolley towards the snaking check-in queue, bent double laughing at the memory of Gemma weeing on the floor in the first week. The girls finally dumped their cases and we set off for the café to have a coffee. "I really am going to miss you all," I said, stirring my drink. We sat in silence, smiling. Sam's phone started ringing.

"Sol? OK. I'll call when I get in. Yep, me too." There had been teary goodbyes at breakfast, but she looked fine now. "That was Sol. He misses me," she said, grinning like a Cheshire cat.

"See – you'll be fine," I said. "He loves you. Nothing to worry about."

We had a massive group hug at the gate and I could feel a few tears coming on. When we pulled away, everyone else was red-eyed too with the effort of not blubbing.

"Make sure you tell us EVERYTHING," Gemma said. "Text us with updates daily!" I waved until I couldn't see them any more.

I felt deflated, but I couldn't help feeling excited at the same time. So much had happened, and yet so much was about to. My first night with Dad that Saturday (if our practice runs were anything to go by, then it would be hilarious), a whole blissful summer with Sex God Matt, the wedding of the century, and best of all, Mum was coming out for a long weekend with her friend Fi. She wanted to see me DJ!

I strolled through the double doors out into the startling sunshine, automatically pulling my sunnies down from my forehead. Lena spotted me and beeped her horn – I was going home.

*Look out for more
brilliant, sexy,
teen-rated reads...*

JUST DON'T LET YOUR LITTLE SISTER GET HER HANDS ON THEM...

footloose

it's the only way to be

When we met Mike said, "That new? God, you look fantastic." He wrapped his arms round me and buried his face in my hair and then he muttered, "You'll have everyone in Greece going after you. I'm so sodding *jealous*, Kelly, I can't bear it. I *wish* you were coming with me."

It was like the words were torn out of him. I forgave him everything on the spot. We told each other that being apart would be awful but that it would make getting together again all the more wonderful.

It was a graceful, forgiving, adult arrangement.

I should have known it wouldn't work out.

kate cann

fiesta

it's a celebration

"I'm Juan," the stranger replies. "The son of Miguel. My father sent me to check you were OK. In all this rain."

I step inside the kitchen. Juan's pulled his hood back, he's shaking back his black hair. The eyes, the nose, the jaw, the *mouth* – everything shifts into perfect balance. He's possibly the most gorgeous, most romantic-looking guy I have ever seen in my whole life.

And beside me I can positively feel Yaz thinking, *OK, Laura – which one of us'll have him?*

kate cann

love
letters

I stood up and was unhooking my bag from the chair when I glanced out of the window. I stopped what I was doing and focused on the college gates. The man in the leather coat was still there. I'd thought he was waiting for a bus, but there were a couple behind him standing at the stop, passengers stepping into them. He'd had his back to me before, but now he was facing me. I knew straight away who he was. He saw me looking and gave a little wave, just a tiny one, his hand in front of his chin. I lifted up the blue paper and envelope, above the neat address the words, BY HAND.

This time he had delivered the love letter himself.

Anne Cassidy

MISSING
judy

Judy Hockney was only five years old when she went missing on a cold November afternoon eight years ago. She was a bright, talkative child, not at all shy. She was with her sister, Kim, on the afternoon that it happened.

I felt the familiar heaviness in my stomach. My dad looked up at me and smiled.

After a quarrel with her sister she walked off and was never seen again. Her mother, Maureen Hockney, searched the streets for her daughter for about fifteen minutes. Then she rang the police. Local officers and neighbours did house-to-house searches, and at first light the following morning the nearby river was searched by police frogmen. There was no trace of Judy.

Anne Cassidy